SOLSTICE OF THE DROWNED EMPIRE

FRANKIE DIANE MALLIS

SEVEN QUEENS PRESS

Cover Designer: Stefanie Saw

Character Art: Tony Viento

Map Art: K.C. Hayes

978-1-957014-05-0Paperback

978-1-957014-06-7Hardback

❀ Created with Vellum

For the readers of Team Forsworn Mayhem, the best Street Team in the world. This is for you, because really, Solstice would not exist without your enthusiasm. You were the first to ask for Rhyan's POV, particularly for the one specific scene that gave this novella its title. And you were also the ones who I'm pretty sure manifested this short story into a novella (shhhh, it's technically a novel with the final word count). Enjoy!

DROWNED EMPIRE SERIES READING ORDER

1. DAUGHTER OF THE DROWNED EMPIRE (DROWNED EMPIRE #1)
2. GUARDIAN OF THE DROWNED EMPIRE (DROWNED EMPIRE #2)
3. SOLSTICE OF THE DROWNED EMPIRE: A DROWNED EMPIRE NOVELLA (DROWNED EMPIRE #0.5)

Please note: the events of this novella take place three years before the main storyline of DAUGHTER, however, SOLSTICE contains spoilers for books 1 and 2.

CONTENT WARNING

SOLSTICE INCLUDES THE FOLLOWING:

Misogyny
  References to sexual assault
  Narcissistic abuse and physical violence
  References to domestic and child abuse
  Ruminations on depression

NIGHT LANDS

GLEMARIA

GRYPHON
MOUN...

ALLURIAN PASS

HARTAVIA SINDHUVINE

EREZTIA

ARAV...

PAYUNMAR

NUMERIA

DAMARA

KORTERIA

THENE

CRETANYA

ELYRIA

VURKSHIRE KEEP

ZAELANDRIA

SCHOLAR'S
BAY

KHEMET

SCHOLAR...
HARBOR

THE L
L

LUMERIAN OCEAN

N

ARAN

LETHEA

GRYPHON ISLAND

...ERIAN EMPIRE
...ERIA NUTAVIA

LUMERIAN OCEAN

N

URION
RTMENTS

SEA TOWER

GRYPHON
ISLAND

GUARDIAN
OF BAMARIA

BAMARIA

THREE YEARS BEFORE DAUGHTER OF THE DROWNED EMPIRE...

CHAPTER
ONE

"Stop slouching, Rhyan. You look like a commoner." My father glared from across the litter, his icy aura biting as he spoke. One hand was tightened around the scroll he'd been reading while the other gripped the hilt of the sword at his waist. Shining black leather covered the handle, which led to a blade he had forced me to sharpen and polish myself under his watch before breakfast.

I'd been trapped inside this litter with him for five fucking hours since, and for days we'd been moving through the sweltering southern heat of the Empire. I wouldn't have necessarily called what my body was doing "slouching," but I'd broken decorum as far as noble posture went and had let myself slip, appearing less than perfect as the son of an Imperator.

A pit formed in my stomach as I tried to assess how angry he was. I couldn't tell. The energy of his rage never matched the degree of what I had or hadn't done. Still, I moved to sit straighter, to roll my shoulders back. It didn't guarantee he wouldn't take further action, but not acquiescing definitely meant he would retaliate. Beads of sweat rolled down the length of my spine as I adjusted myself, and I fought the urge to wipe them away and scratch at the itch increasing beneath my tunic under his careful watch.

But even as the temperature continued to rise, the suffocating heat was nothing to the auric stab of ice provided by my father, Arkasva Hart, High Lord of Glemaria, Imperator to the North, one of the three most powerful men in the Empire of Lumeria.

"Rhyan, you are Heir Apparent to Ka Hart, the noblest of Kavim. You're nineteen years old, three months away from participating in the Revelation Ceremony. Three months away from becoming useful in this Godsdamned society. By the Gods, learn to act like it."

Or else. The unspoken threat, always present behind his words, sliced through me. His aura expanded, so cold it burned as painfully as the sun beating down on our travels. From a stab of ice it had grown to a full-on storm that forced me to sit back in my seat.

Despite the freeze, I was no cooler than I'd been before. Every word out of his mouth, every mention of my upcoming Revelation Ceremony, was a lie he maintained for the sake of appearances. And every mention of it made me want to crawl out of my skin, made me feel like I was going to burst with insanity. As if I didn't already want to explode with rage at any given moment of the day.

My power, my magic, my strength as a soturion—a warrior of Lumeria—had been bound inside of me only moments after it had been revealed in an early, secret ceremony.

The unbinding had taken place on the morning of my nineteenth birthday at the stark end of winter. Snow had still coated the grounds of Glemaria, though the temperature had risen significantly. Instead of wishing me a happy birthday or celebrating the fact that I was eligible to participate in the next Revelation Ceremony, coming into both my title as Heir Apparent and my power, he'd declared I was old enough for the blade, ready to take any additional punishments—or *lessons* as he liked to call them—like a man.

As if to prove he was stronger than me even with my power unleashed, he'd decided I was to be unbound early. Illegally. But when you were second in power to the Emperor of Lumeria, some rules didn't apply. For every other nineteen-year-old of the Empire, this ceremony was to be performed at the end of summer and before witnesses—before an Imperator. Technically, I supposed, we'd fulfilled that part of the obligation.

My father had brought Glemaria's ancient Arkmage into my bedroom to perform the ceremony. I'd thought I'd still have months to go before I'd be cut, before I'd make the choice to become a soturion and earn my blade. I'd thought I'd be doing this alongside my friends, the future Soturi of Ka Glemaria. But, as usual, I'd been alone.

The Arkmage had had a dagger ready for me before my eyes had been fully cleared of sleep. He'd made the slice to my left arm, my blood dripping into the bowl of fire the old man had conjured as I'd said the words and the Birth Bind had been removed. The first part of my oath complete.

It had taken only seconds for it to happen. For the worst to come. For my vorakh to reveal itself.

Forbidden magic. Cursed. Taboo. A blight. An embarrassment. Vorakh was the only magic absolutely illegal in the Empire, the kind of magic that rogue hunters pursued. And I'd been "gifted" with the worst of the three. The one that was most impossible to hide when it revealed itself.

Not mind reading. Not seeing visions. I could travel—appear and reappear anywhere at any time, but without any control.

As if my father had needed another reason to despise me, needed another thing to find wrong with me, or another basis for his belief that I was a plague on his name, on our Ka. The moment the golden light of the Birth Bind had disappeared, my body had vanished from his sight and reappeared, leaving me dizzy and nauseated. Terror had raced through my veins before I could process what had happened, before I could let my father's hateful words sink in.

And then, just like that, I was gone.

One second, I'd been in my bedroom, and the next, my stomach had twisted, and I'd found myself on the cliffs of the mountains behind the fortress, my bare feet crunching in the snow beside a pack of sleeping gryphons. Next, I'd traveled to a stranger's home in an empty living room with a roaring fire, the sounds of a family preparing breakfast in the adjoining kitchen. I'd then returned to under my father's roof, sweating, scared, on the verge of vomiting, and confused as to how I'd traveled so quickly. I hadn't known what to do, how to stop it from happening again.

I had been terrified of being discovered, terrified it would happen again, terrified of where my body would fall next. But I couldn't move, my limbs were shaking, my muscles raw. Exhaustion had taken over me almost immediately, and I'd collapsed to my knees before I'd been able to assess my surroundings, retreat, or escape.

My father's guards had been everywhere, searching every inch of the fortress and its grounds for me. They'd bound me in rope and dragged me before my Arkasva and Imperator in the Seating Room where he'd perched on his golden chair like it truly was a throne. He'd told everyone I'd ran away that morning, that I was a coward who feared becoming a man on my birthday. Only three of us had known the truth: me, him, and the Arkmage. Only the three of us had known I had vorakh. A secret that was deadly. If anyone else—like Emperor Theotis—ever learned of it, I would be executed. So would my father.

The thought, I hated to admit, was almost appealing. Almost. Despite my hatred for him, I wasn't ready to sacrifice my life to end his. Not yet.

The Emperor had executed an entire Ka years earlier for

concealing a vorakh in their family. Ka Azria, the noble rulers in the south, had been a warning across Lumeria, though not one I'd ever thought *I'd* have to heed. But now it was, and on that morning, I knew what my father was thinking because for once, I was thinking it, too.

We could be next.

I'd barely been unbound a quarter of an hour before he'd forced the Arkmage to put the Birth Bind back on, trapping my magic inside me. This reversal spell was not commonly—or ever, really—done, but it had been my father's order, and so the Arkmage had done it. And then my father had made the Arkmage swear to tell no one on pain of death.

"I will take this secret to my grave, your highness," he'd said, his eyes pleading.

"Yes, you will," my father had said calmly.

When he'd pulled out a dagger, I'd expected him to make us all swear a blood oath.

He'd put the blade through the Arkmage's heart instead before ordering me to get dressed and attend my birthday breakfast as if nothing had happened. Over eggs and coffee, he'd told his court of the tragic passing of the ancient man. And that had been that. A new Arkmage had been anointed by nightfall. We'd never spoken of it again.

I hated the lie. Hated how unaffected my father had been. Hated how for months, I'd lain awake at night, itching and feeling farther than Lethea with the power that had been unleashed and so quickly trapped back inside me.

Now, as he stared from across the litter, I bit the inside of my cheek, pushing my shoulders back farther and puffing my chest up. His dark eyebrows narrowed to a V as he watched me—judged me—but he said nothing.

I felt my skin crawling, just waiting for his next insult, his next command, his next—

"Better, your highness?" I asked, unable to stand the tension.

The deep lines around his mouth deepened as he frowned, his eyes continuing to assess my posture. "Were you addressed just now?" His thumb stroked the sword's hilt at his waist, a gentler caress than I'd ever seen him use on anyone or anything with a living, beating heart.

I coughed. "No, your highness."

"Then shut your mouth."

My lips pursed, but I did as my Arkasva, as my Imperator bid. I shut my mouth as I stared at the green velvet curtains embroidered with silver gryphons covering each of our windows. These windows were my only means of escape, my only source of anything to look at besides my father's hateful face, and I'd been denied. Instead of seeing the southern countryside, watching each country pass by, I was staring at the same curtains that adorned every window in his fortress back home. Worse, the curtains trapped in the heat and cut off any semblance of a breeze that passed through. I was ready to crawl out of my skin. A scream had been building deep inside me for hours, and if I didn't get out of here soon, I would go crazy.

But I had to stay calm. I couldn't upset him.

My life had been shrunken down to these four small walls for weeks, all thanks to my father's obsession with making an impression and cultivating his every appearance. If we'd flown on gryphons like I'd wanted to, we'd have crossed the Empire in days with our soturi moving quickly behind us. And I'd have been free—flying, feeling the wind, able to breathe and see the sky above me without walls. But my father believed any old Lumerian could dominate an animal—it was dominating people that made one strong. So gryphons were out of the question.

Not even the threat of facing akadim on the road curtailed him. As he said, these ancient monsters were all in the north, and we were traveling south, away from them in their least favorite season. And let the beasts try!

The entire journey was farther than Lethea. Arkasvim didn't even travel by litter across their own countries.

I tapped a finger against my leg, focusing on the movement, the feeling, the fabric of my black linen tunic, and the *tap tap tap* sound, trying desperately to distract myself from the sweat rolling down my nape, the itch spreading across my legs beneath my boots, and the twisting in my stomach.

If he'd at least open a Godsdamned window, let me breathe, let me see something new for fucking once…but he wouldn't. Gods forbid a menial nobody of the Lumerian Empire see the Imperator without his permission. Gods forbid I enjoy myself for a fucking minute. He was suffering, too. I knew it. Even he couldn't command his aura to keep him cool for an entire day in the heat. And my aura…mine was trapped, imprisoned, suffocating, cut off thanks to the bind. Of course, we had mages who could cool us off, we even had windows we could open! But my suffering was worth far more than his comfort. He got off on it.

I stared helplessly at the walls imprisoning me. Nothing to do, nothing to see. No way to escape. I'd brought scrolls to read and help me pass the endless hours of our journey, but even at our sickeningly slow-and-steady pace, I felt nauseated every time I tried to read, so they sat uselessly beside me, rolling back and forth across the bench, still sealed in their leather cases.

My father's eyes flicked to my leg from the half-read scroll in his lap, and immediately, my finger stilled. Had I angered him? The tapping hadn't made much noise. And my posture hadn't shifted. Had he remembered some past offense—or rather, some past offense he'd conjured?

"What is that face you're wearing?" He reached for his belt, his fingers tracing the hilt of his dagger. I stopped breathing, but then his hand slid along the leather strap, opening a pouch beside his sword, removing a green silk handkerchief. He wiped it across his forehead though I doubted it did him much good. He'd sweat so much the cloth was soaked.

I lifted my eyebrows in mock surprise. "Why, I'm wearing the face I was born with, your highness."

"Do you think you are clever?"

I bit the inside of my cheek. Fuck. I was too tired and over-heated to watch my mouth. My only reprieves on this trip had been pissing off the side of the road every few hours. I'd drunk an excess of coffee the first day to prompt such breaks, but he'd caught on and made me wait so long I'd feared I'd wet myself in front of him. As if I wasn't suffering enough holding my magic in, he'd made me hold my piss. Since then, I'd erred on the side of caution, barely hydrating at all and only when he did. He, at least, relieved himself whenever he wanted. My Imperator did whatever he wanted.

"I must have misunderstood the question," I said, praying my voice sounded even. Not scared, not confrontational.

"Your mother passed that face off to you when you ripped your way out her cunt. I see none of myself." The edges of his lips quirked as if he were amused, and then, like a strike of light-ning, his body shot forward, his large hand already formed into a fist.

I shut my eyes. A reflex, born of years of practice. My body stiffened and stomach tightened, and I recalled something pleas-ant. My last night in Glemaria. Reading alone in my bedroom for a full hour in peace. Spiced mead in my cup. A fire roaring. My blankets soft.

Inhale...exhale....

Just like that, it was over.

My eyes sprang open, and I blinked back tears. I wheezed, coughing before I could help myself.

It had been a punch to my stomach this time. Always below the face. Always where no one could see. Arms and legs were fair game back home, but since our visit to the south meant less clothing, he'd taken to aiming at my torso. Bandages covered the black and blue marks on my back thanks to my most recent whipping. My ribcage was still tender from last night. But I'd learned to present myself as if I were without injury. To an outsider, I looked perfectly unharmed.

He narrowed his dark eyebrows, his nostrils flaring, red as his overly heated forehead, and some small part of me withered. I was supposed to be stronger than this. I wasn't that boy anymore. Helpless, powerless. I never would be again. I was of age in Lumeria. A man by law even without having completed the Revelation Ceremony, even with my power trapped. I had been of age for months. I had powerful magic. Strength inside me.

Anger boiled within. And then I released it.

I didn't have power.

The idea that I did—that was the myth I told myself. It didn't matter if I was nineteen or nine. I couldn't fight him. He was too strong. I didn't stand a chance before my official Revelation Ceremony came and he had no choice but to unbind me. Until my strength as a warrior was unbound and unleashed, I could do nothing to him. Especially when he kept my sword and dagger captive.

But even then, with my strength unleashed, my fingers curled around the hilt of a sword…what would I do?

He'd still be my father. The Arkasva, ruler of my country, Glemaria. The golden borders of his black cloak marked him as Imperator of the North, second in power only to the Emperor. He ruled over half the Empire of Lumeria, was an expertly trained soturion, a deadly warrior, and had the entire country and army under his thumb.

If he didn't kill me one day, someone who discovered I was vorakh would. I was fucked.

I swallowed roughly, feelings of hopelessness and dread of my future washing over me. I'd never escape. My life was worthless. I might as well live in this litter. There was no good outcome for me, no matter which way I looked. I could just end—

No. I wouldn't entertain those thoughts. I had reasons to live. I was just...far away from them.

He sat back, pulling out his disgusting handkerchief and swiping it across his fist before carefully examining his fingers as if he might have dirtied them when punching me.

He replaced the cloth again, his dark eyes running up and down my body.

"You see how you anger me?" His voice was calm, full of sincere concern. "Whatever you look like, Rhyan, you are still my son. My blood. I gave you the name of my Ka. I want to see you be successful, the future of Glemaria, just like I taught you since you were a boy." He sighed, as if deeply troubled. "But you make me so uncertain of you. How can I believe in you until you show some true strength? Prove to me that you can handle the curse placed upon you? I don't want to doubt you, but you're so intent on causing me to do so. It's as if you want me to lose faith in you. I don't want to, you know that, but these childish antics of yours leave me no choice. For your own safety, I may have to keep you bound forever."

My bottom lip quivered, and I spoke out only to hide it. "I shall try harder, your highness." I realized with horror he really might do as he threatened. I'd go mad.

His eyes filled with concern. If I didn't know what kind of monster he was deep down, I'd feel sorry for him. Sorry for *him*, when *he* punched *me*. I knew logically it wasn't my fault. I hadn't forced his hand. How could I have? I'd never had any say in his decisions or any impact on their outcome. He was Imperator. Arkasva. I was not.

Yet my heart couldn't tell the difference. Neither could my body, my soul. I tensed again under his gaze, his words repeating in my mind.

"You flinched!" he roared. "Flinched just from looking at

me. You better not flinch before the court of Bamaria. You hear me?"

I inhaled. Slowly. Very slowly. Not here. Not now. I was not going to lose control. Not in front of him. Not because of him. We were so close to Bamaria, to this part of the trip, this torture, being over.

My stomach tensed, some of the pain dulling. "I think it was a bump in the road," I said, casually. "We're in Elyria, aren't we? Hard to tell when the scenery never changes." I stared at my hand, curling my fingers and pretending to inspect beneath my nails for dirt. "You'd think Ka Elys might use their taxes to repair these roads at some point. Full of holes."

"You really think yourself so clever, don't you?" His hand flew, his fist connecting with the cushion beside my face. "That's your last warning."

My heart pounded. Inhale...exhale....

He'll blame you if you're hit, it'll be your fault. It's always your fault. Because you're too fucking weak, too foolish, too stupid, too childish to navigate this better. Too powerless to escape. To leave. To...to fight back.

I tried to bury my thoughts, my feelings, push them so far down I'd never have to face them again. But they kept swimming back to the surface.

"We're fucking floating on the shoulders of servants," my father snarled. "There are no bumps in the road."

I shrugged, willing my heart to stop drumming so loudly.

There were certainly bumps in the road, but I supposed if you were too noble to touch the ground, it didn't matter how battered a servant's boots might be by now.

"Myself to Moriel, Rhyan, if you don't think I won't make it so you can't sit for a week."

My stomach churned. I'd be expected at all sorts of state dinners with Arkasva Batavia and his daughters. No doubt, my father would relish watching me squirm in pain as I sat through each function.

"Your highness," I said, bowing my chin in respect. It was the heat. It had to be heat making him extra irritable. Not me. Not anything I'd done. The trip would be over soon, I'd be all right. It would all be all right.

"Don't *your highness* me! You think I'm so easily appeased?"

"No, your highness," I said, carefully.

Distantly, I heard the nearest Elyrian clocktowers shouting the time. How many more hours must I endure this? How much longer could I stand to be trapped in here with him?

"Should have left you home," he said.

I wished he had. I'd have given anything to not have taken this trip. To not have been so close to him. To have had weeks without his presence looming over me like a constant shadow, his guards spying on me every hour of the day, waiting to report some minor misstep, some word spoken out of turn.

Gods forbid he left me home with Mother, left me to enjoy an entire summer of his absence, not fall victim to his every mood swing. To stay in a fortress with open windows and a cool summer breeze blowing in from the mountains. To ride gryphons freely. For my moods to be my own and not his.

To just fucking breathe.

No amount of wishing or dreaming would change that.

An Afeya might. We'd passed an encampment from the Sun Court back in Damara. I used to be terrified of the stories told about the immortal beings from Lumeria Matavia. The way they'd trick you into deals, offer you a wish granted only for you to pay a price too horrible to name in return, like being given the love of your life only for your heart to shrivel up the day you met her.

A shriveled heart didn't sound so bad right about now. Dead hearts couldn't be broken.

At least my mother had a summer to be free. I had to be grateful for that. She deserved it. She deserved more, but at least that. She was safe. She would get a break. At least my being here distracted him from her.

"The will of the Imperator is the will of the north," I said. "I am your humble servant and will return home at once if you believe that is where I should be."

My father shook his head, his graying black hair cut severely close to his scalp. The golden Laurel of the Arkasva wreathed around his forehead. "Sit up," he demanded again, even though he was slouching far worse than I had been.

He pulled at the leathered armor around his neck in an attempt to cool off. If he stopped being so Godsdamned farther than Lethea, he might actually suffer less. His aura often froze me at home in the fortress where temperatures dropped into the negative degrees half of winter, but here, in the south when I needed his cold and so did he—nothing. Godsdamned fucking bastard.

I sat up as he commanded. My posture was perfect though my hands twitched in my lap.

"Before the Bamarian Council, you will address me as Father."

I gestured at the walls of our litter and the empty benches beside us. We were not before the Bamarian Council.

His hand flew up. "Say it, Rhyan. I need to be sure your cursed and feeble mind is capable of completing this small, menial task. Show me. Show me you're smart enough for this."

I stared back, my lips sealed shut. He did not deserve the name. He had done nothing to merit the title. I felt sick, sick with heat, sick of his face, sick of his threats, sick to my stomach where he'd punched me. At least that was empty, or I'd have been puking.

I glanced around the litter. I did not want to give him this win when there was no point other than satisfying his Godsdamned ego.

But, as usual, when it came to him, I had no choice.

"Father," I said at last, the word stiff and unfamiliar on my tongue.

"Good boy," he said. And slapped my cheek. "That was for hesitating. Now try to rest. We'll be arriving soon and expected to appear before all of Bamaria."

As if nothing had happened, he began humming and returned to reading his scroll.

I closed my eyes, praying I'd either fall asleep or successfully feign a nap. Preferably sleep, but it was too fucking hot in the south.

~

T wo hours later, we approached the Bamarian border. Finally ready to greet an audience, my father used his aura to blast cool air through the litter. The look of relief in his eyes was palpable until he caught sight of me and frowned. But, at last, I didn't feel like I was going to die from heat stroke, and—thank the Gods—he pulled back the curtains of our litter. A sharp gust from his aura dried any sweat stains on my tunic, removed any body odor, and dissipated the sweat beading at my neck and behind my calves. He even used his power to dry my hair and twist my locks into perfect little curls. Auriel's bane. As if we'd had the most pleasant, luxurious ride the Empire had ever seen.

I immediately ran my hand through my hair to undo the curls, but a sharp look from my Arkasva made me still. Coifed Heir Apparent it was.

Before the gates of Bamaria, half a dozen soturi stepped forward. Every single soturion was male. What in Lumeria? The Soturi of Ka Batavia had always been equal between genders.

Even more alarming, each soturion wore silver armor, the metal styled to appear like the pelt of a wolf. Bamarian soturi wore golden armor.

My heart sank, and tears burned behind my eyes.

These were the Soturi of Ka Kormac.

No. Gods, no. If we were in Korteria, I was going to scream. Not only was its ruler, Imperator Kormac, an insufferable snake, but to be in Korteria meant we still had another week of traveling ahead. I had calculated we'd end our journey today based on us following a strictly southeast route. Had we been going west while I'd stared at green curtains? Fuck! Fuck! I wasn't going to survive another week of this.

"Welcome to Bamaria, Imperator," said the closest soturion, bowing low. He had black, beady eyes that half the wolves from Korteria seemed to possess. "Your highness, Imperator Hart, we are honored to greet you."

I frowned, confused but relieved as I was introduced, all while I remained still and in perfect posture with my perfectly curled hair and even more perfect manners. My face remained in a practiced expression of disdain, as the usual formalities were conducted. We were greeted, we were bowed to, the whole boring spectacle. When Ka Kormac's simpering wolves had praised the northern Imperator long enough, we were allowed passage through the gates and offered a Bamarian escort to accompany our party to their fortress.

The moment our litter began to progress again, my father shut the curtains. "Wolves at the gates of seraphim country. They should be ashamed," he muttered. But the edges of his mouth lifted into a cruel smile. He was positively gleeful. "But a rather fascinating study, I should think."

I racked my mind for an explanation, for some reason why soturi of a foreign Ka would have greeted us at the Bamarian border.

Our litter lurched forward, and I slid out of my posture,

watching my father to see if he'd noticed. His eyes were on me as usual, and before I could think, I blurted out, "Why is Ka Kormac greeting us? This isn't their country."

I stiffened, knowing he was just as likely to yell or hit me again as he was to answer me. But, for once, I was lucky, and he grinned wider, looking excited to answer the question.

"Arkasva Batavia is an incompetent and impotent fool."

Arkasva Batavia had come to the Seat of Power in Bamaria over fifteen years earlier. Sixteen? I needed to brush up on my Bamarian history. I only knew he'd taken the Seat after his wife, Marianna Batavia, the High Lady of Bamaria, had passed. And though this was a fairly regular practice across the Empire, in Bamaria this had been highly unusual. Women of Ka Batavia only passed the Laurel of the Arkasva to another woman of the maternal bloodline. This made Bamaria the only country of the Empire to have been ruled exclusively by women—until now. There'd been some civil unrest and a small rebellion after it had happened, but it had been quashed, and the High Lord of Bamaria remained in power.

"He has a lame leg," my father said conspiratorially with a sparkle in his eyes.

"I remember from our last visit, your highness." I was met with a glare and quickly amended, "Father."

"Yes. You were five?"

"Ten." But he well knew that. He was trying to bait me.

"Watch your accent," he said. "You sound ridiculous. Childish and uneducated."

I sounded like I was from the north. From Glemaria, to be exact. Like everyone else back home. Every tutor, every teacher had taught me to "speak properly" to minimize the accent that signified my country of origin.

My father did not have a Glemarian accent. Despite many familial ties to Glemaria, he hadn't been born there. My mother had. My father was originally from Hartavia, one of our northern border countries.

"Yes, Father," I said, using the practiced "proper" accent he preferred. The one that didn't come from our true home. The one that didn't remind him he was the foreigner. The one that didn't remind him that my mother had more nobility in her bloodline than he ever would.

I felt the litter still sometime later. Once more, my father's aura lashed out, quick and sharp. Again, he used it to ensure I was cool, looked like a proper Heir Apparent, and that everything about my presence and appearance would impress the Bamarian Council and court.

The floor shifted beneath me, and at last, our litter was set on the ground. A mage in my father's service wound back the curtains, and I looked out the window to see the fortress of Bamaria for the first time in years.

Cresthaven was massive, designed in glittering blue mosaic tiles that gave the impression it was rising from the waves of the Lumerian Ocean, or maybe was part of the water itself. I could already smell the salt clinging to the air and the warm breeze I'd felt all those years ago on our last visit.

The Soturi of Ka Hart, outfitted in black leathered armor with golden Valalumir stars shining on their belts, filed up to the entrance of Cresthaven where two soturi of Ka Batavia stood guard. They wore golden armor that curved over their shoulders shaped into sharpened seraphim wings. The giant birds were beloved in Bamaria, used for travel, and formed the sigil of Ka Batavia—golden seraphim wings beneath a silver full moon.

Ka Hart was opposite in design. Our armor was covered in black leather—necessary for the Glemarian winters—and our sigil showcased silver gryphon wings beneath a golden sun.

Bells rang out, and I stared up at the clouds, half expecting to see gryphons taking flight for the hourly patrol of the border. Every hour on the hour, riders released the creatures from their bonds and took them to the sky for exercise while searching up north for enemies and, more importantly, akadim.

I almost felt homesick when the massive brown and gray gryphon wings did not appear. Instead, the sky filled with glowing blue lights beneath the hooves of ashvan horses. Right…they rode ashvan here for patrol.

My father turned to me with a warning look in his eyes as the doors opened.

"Fix your diadem," he snarled. With a jerk of his chin, an escort from his personal guard marched over and produced a mirror from his bag, holding it before my face.

I glanced at my reflection. The diadem was on perfectly. Silver gryphon wings laid across my forehead vanished into my curls, bronze beneath the sunlight. Centered above my eyes, which he'd said were "strangely green," was a golden sun. I was the perfect image of Ka Hart. Minus my too-green eyes.

"Stop gaping at yourself. Not much to see when you've been given the looks of your mother. The vanity of an Heir Apparent, I swear," my father said, and with a chuckle, he dismissed the escort.

He knew damn well the diadem was on correctly. He was just trying to humiliate me, to find some way to unsettle me without a hit before our grand entrance.

I sealed my mouth shut, wishing I were anywhere but here, knowing I didn't have it in me to smile or be cordial by this hour of the day. I would simply be, and they'd all think, WHAT a horrible, miserable HEIR, and I didn't have enough left in me to give a shit.

My boots touched the inside of Cresthaven's Grand Hall, an impressive room of columns painted with stories of the ancient arkasvim of Bamaria. Unlike Glemaria, which had warring factions and different Kavim taking power back from each other every few centuries, Bamaria had remained steadfast in the hands of Ka Batavia's female bloodline.

Until now. Was that why Ka Kormac was here?

The heralds shouted our arrival into the hall, which was empty. We were to be greeted in the Seating Room personally by Arkasva Batavia, his heirs, and the Bamarian Council.

Sun shining in through the massive windows of the hall left a dazzling array of color across the marble floor until, suddenly, the room darkened. Or, rather, something brighter caught my eye. A splash of red, glowing bright as fire.

Two noblewomen, around my age, raced down the stairs leading into the Great Hall. The one in front had loose brown waves running down her back, thick like a lion's mane. She tugged along the noblewoman behind her, her face screwed up in concentration.

"Sorry!" she yelled, her bright eyes widening as she spotted us. "Running late." She jumped down to the bottom step, motioning for the second noble behind her to follow. "Lyr! Come on!"

My throat went dry as I saw her. As I watched her jump.

Lyr.

Lady Lyriana Batavia, the third daughter of Arkasva Batavia.

She seemed to glow as her feet touched the ground. She wore a small victorious grin, as if happy she'd made the leap. But the smile vanished as she turned and raced down the hall. Her deep, lustrous brown hair had turned red with flames right before my eyes.

I stared at her retreating figure, suddenly anxious, ready to enter Cresthaven, to follow her. My gaze did, at the very least, as my father harumphed at the disrespect and lack of decorum.

Once she was gone, the lights in the hall seemed to return, and the sun shined brighter than it had a moment before. We were led forward into the Great Hall where she had just stood only a minute ago. My heart pounded, and I closed my eyes.

All I could see was red.

CHAPTER
TWO

Red. I'd nearly forgotten. Lady Lyriana, or Lyr, as her sisters and cousin called her, had been a child on my last visit. Well, to be fair, so had I. But I'd thought it had meant something important at the time—made me a bigger deal than I was—because my age had been in the double digits. I'd been ten, and I believe that would have made her seven. But, truly, growing up as heirs to the arkasva, there would have been very little difference between our experiences and education thus far. We were both just kids.

I'd spent half the trip completely ignoring her simply because she was seven. But I'd found myself noticing her every time she'd entered the room for no reason I could put my finger on. I had been too young to feel attraction or any real interest in girls. But I'd noticed her. Every time. Noticed her smile, noticed her laugh. Found myself thinking about her when she wasn't around. Nothing that could be considered inappropriate—I didn't even know what those thoughts were. I had simply wondered where she was, what she was doing, thinking. I'd had this feeling from the moment I'd met her that I'd known her. I'd felt safe around her.

Which hadn't made any sense at the time, and still didn't.

Even when I felt that magnetic pull to seek her out again and again.

My mind sifted through my memories of that first visit. She had always been with her cousin, the Lady Julianna Batavia. Jules. The girls of Ka Batavia all had nicknames for each other. I remembered that now. I'd been jealous. I'd had no one I could refer to by a nickname. No one I was that close to.

Jules was probably who'd been pulling her down the stairs just then. Lady Julianna wasn't in line to the Seat of Power—not an heir of Ka Batavia. Her forehead had been bare while Lady Lyriana had worn a golden circlet across hers, the golden chains of her diadem vanishing into her red hair.

Fuck. She'd grown up. And she was…beautiful. Stunning.

I remembered the one and only afternoon I'd spent alone with her. I'd nearly forgotten, but being here, seeing her again, it all came rushing back.

Father had been in a horrific mood that day. That was true every day, but that one had been particularly brutal. His aura had blasted like a hurricane at me. I'd been so small at the time I'd stumbled backward, my backside hitting a desk that had left a bruise for days. I'd thought for sure, everyone in Cresthaven had to notice, had to feel it. I'd been embarrassed, worried I'd caused a scene and would get in even more trouble. And yet…no one had come. No one had said or done anything. Just like at home. The floors of the fortress had been shaking with his rage, and…nothing.

I didn't remember what I'd done wrong. I wasn't sure I'd even known at the time. I might have breathed the wrong way, might have looked at him funny. It rarely ever mattered.

One of our personal guards had knocked on the door, and I'd used the opportunity to run, fleeing from the guest wing of Cresthaven, wishing I hadn't been Heir Apparent, wishing I hadn't been Glemarian, wishing I hadn't had a father.

I'd run in circles, up and down halls without any care for

where I was or the fact that I was utterly and completely lost. Somehow, I found myself in the heir's wing, rounding down a long hallway. One door had been wide open. I'd planned on sneaking by, assuming someone had been in there and I'd be in trouble for going into the heir's private quarters. I'd guessed it was one of the ladies playing in their bedroom, but then I'd smelled something sweet. Cake.

Lemon cake. I'd been hungry. I didn't remember why. I sometimes didn't eat, not because I was ever starved—he hadn't thought of that cruelty—I just sometimes felt too sick to eat. Or the food I was served didn't appeal to me. But I'd been hungry then, and so I'd stopped in the doorway, curious to see if I could take a slice with me as I searched for a hiding spot, a place to feel safe for a few hours before my father found me again.

When I'd peeked around the door, I'd found it wasn't a bedroom, but a library. Shelves of scrolls, some bare, some in shining leather cases, had adorned the walls from floor to ceiling between ocean-facing windows that had opened onto balconies. In the room's center had been two red velvet couches and a circular table between them.

Lady Lyriana had been sitting on one of the couches, her legs propped up on the cushions and feet bare, as she'd read a scroll with an intensity unusual for a seven-year-old. A lemon cake and a decanter of water had sat on the small table, and on a smaller golden plate by her foot had been a half-eaten slice, white icing dripping down the center. The sound of the ocean had coursed through the room, the waves rolling back and forth, birds calling as they flew past the windows.

"Lord Rhyan, your grace," she had said clumsily as she'd looked up, startled to see me.

I'd shaken my head at her, angered she'd noticed my presence. Angered I'd revealed weakness—or so I'd thought at the time. I'd imagined everyone could see what an embarrassment I was.

Now, I knew I most likely looked like any other ten-year-old boy of Lumerian nobility. Like a kid.

"What is this?" I'd asked, my voice full of scorn, full of the hatred for my father I'd been unable to express.

"It's our personal library," she'd said, her voice small.

"Don't heir's wings have nurseries?"

Lady Lyriana had narrowed her eyes. "It did...but we're too old. So, it's a library now."

"And this is what you do in your free time?"

Her lips had pursed together. "I'm reading," she'd snapped. And with that, her gaze had returned to the scroll in her hands, her fingers tightening around the parchment, knuckles nearly white.

I hadn't been sure what to make of that. Had she been angry with me? Had I embarrassed her? I'd been genuinely curious.

"Reading what?" I'd finally asked, unable to help myself.

"A scroll," she'd said like I was the simplest person in Lumeria.

I'd rolled my eyes. "I can see that. What scroll are you reading?"

"Why do you want to know?"

"Why don't you want to tell me?"

Her almond-shaped eyes had narrowed into snake-like slits. "Because you haven't heard of it."

"How do you know what I have or haven't heard of?"

"Because it's a Bamarian author."

I'd stepped farther into the room. "We have scrolls by Bamarian authors in the Glemarian libraries."

"Oh." She looked back up at me. "I guess you would. We have Glemarian authors here, too." Her manner had changed completely. She'd sounded curious, and interested in talking to me.

But I'd frowned at her response, and she'd looked back down at her scroll, shifting uncomfortably in her seat.

I hadn't known any Glemarian authors. I'd liked reading. A lot. It had helped distract me, helped me pass hours alone. But I'd tended to dive straight into the story; I'd never thought to look at who'd written a scroll before.

I'd taken another step in and another, not wanting to leave. Feeling that odd magnetic pull towards her. I had been fascinated, had wanted to stay. Just wanted to be in the same room as her.

Lyriana's eyes had flicked between me and the scroll, almost hesitantly. I'd waited for her to order me away. Heirs in other countries we'd visited had done just that when they'd tired of me and my foul moods. And, technically, I hadn't been supposed to be in her private quarters to begin with.

But she hadn't dismissed me. She'd sat up in her seat and smoothed her dress over her legs, her jewelry making a pretty jingling sound as she'd shifted, before gesturing to the table, her eyes curious once again. "I have a second copy. Jules was going to read it with me today, but she's not here. She's with my sisters. They all got to go into the city. But Father said I was too...." She'd frowned then seemed to remember I was there and straightened her shoulders. "You could read with me if you want. I'm on chapter three. But you're," she'd scrunched up her nose in concentration, "you're ten, right?"

At this, I'd puffed out my chest and nodded.

She'd bitten her lip, looking down, her expression filled with worry. "So that means you probably read faster than I do. You can let me know when you catch up."

I'd moved slowly across the library, still wary of being kicked out. But I had been asked to stay. And honestly, it had sounded like fun—to sit and read the same story as someone and talk about it and not be nobles, just kids reading. I had been even more excited that it had been *her* inviting me.

I'd sat down on the couch across from Lyriana and picked up

the spare scroll, my hand shaking with excitement and fear she'd tell me she had been kidding. But she'd only smiled.

I tried to remember the story I'd read that day, the title of the scroll, the name of the author, but my mind was empty. I remembered clearly opening to the first chapter as she'd put her scroll down and pushed the lemon cake on the table toward me, the charms and beads on her bracelets chiming again. "Do you like snacks when you read?"

I hadn't liked anything. But I'd been hungry. The cake had drawn me there to begin with.

"It's lemon. My favorite," she'd said. "Morgs and Jules prefer chocolate cake. I like chocolate, too," she'd added quickly as if admitting she hadn't liked chocolate as much as her sister and cousin had been some sort of betrayal on her part. "Do you like lemon?" she asked.

"I do."

She looked unsure of my answer. "Do you, um, do you have lemon trees in Glemaria?"

I'd nodded. "Not many lemons grow there except in the green houses. But we have Bamarian lemons shipped regularly." I'd known this only after being forced to sit in on my father's Glemarian Council meetings. There'd been a brief discussion of importing Bamarian lemons and the cost of doing so. I'd been bored to tears at the time, but felt my knowledge in that moment impressive.

"Oh," she'd said. "Okay. Tell me when you catch up to my chapter."

I'd settled onto the second couch, and I'd eaten a piece of lemon cake. And then another. And it had been the best thing I'd ever tasted in my life because it had been the first time I'd been able to eat without being judged, without being watched. Lady Lyriana had gone back to reading, her eyes intense and focused on the scroll. At one point, a servant had entered with a fresh pitcher of water, and she'd asked if they'd bring in a second glass for me.

Thoughtful. Thoughtful in a way most heirs hadn't been with me before.

And that had been it. We hadn't interacted after that. We'd sat together silently, comfortably, reading for hours with a table and cake between us. I'd finished the scroll in that time. She'd been right—I had read fast. But I'd been distracted. Distracted by her. Distracted by how peaceful I'd felt there, how safe. Distracted by how nice it had been to sit in the same room as someone else that seemed kind and had included me. Distracted by how nice it had been to sit there without pressure as the waves of the ocean lapped back and forth outside and her bracelets rang softly whenever she turned her scroll to read the next page.

Distracted that it was her.

I'd wanted to tell her when I'd reached chapter three, like she'd asked, but she'd seemed so engrossed, I hadn't wanted to disturb her. When I'd finished reading, I'd been worried she'd ask me questions about the story I wouldn't have been able to answer because I hadn't been paying close enough attention. So, I'd rerolled my scroll and been about to start over when my personal escort found me.

"Your grace." His soturion body had been full of height and muscle that had seemed to take up the entire doorway. His Glemarian accent had been heavy, almost embarrassingly so.

Lady Lyriana had looked up, confused, her eyebrows wrinkled until she'd realized the soturion from Glemaria in black leather was there for me, not her.

"Your grace, pardon the intrusion. I was sent to find the little lord," he'd said, bowing to her. His eyes had glazed over the room, taking in our mirrored positions on the couch, the scrolls, and the lemon cake, and my stomach had sunk as if I'd done something wrong. Like I'd be punished for having enjoyed myself, for having cake, for reading, for fun.

Disappointment had washed over me knowing my time with Lyriana had ended. I hadn't expected something like that to happen again.

"Your father has been looking for you. As have I." There had been clear annoyance in his eyes. "Come."

Without a word, I'd gotten up and left. I'd spent the remainder of my time in Bamaria too afraid to tell Lady Lyriana that sitting in silence in her tiny library while reading with lemon cake in my stomach had been the best time I'd ever spent in my ten years of existence. And that sitting there with her, not talking but sharing a story, had been the closest thing to what I'd thought having a friend felt like at the time. But she had been seven, and I had been ten, and…it had all seemed pathetic and laughable, and we were leaving soon anyway and probably not visiting again, so what had it mattered?

Nine years later, I remembered the scent of lemon cake and the way her expressions had so clearly reflected what she'd read. I'd known when she was reading a funny moment even though she hadn't laughed out loud, and I'd known when the story had become serious and full of tension.

My father glared at me from the corner of his eye now, back in the Great Hall of Cresthaven. I swallowed, straightened, and slowed my step. Had I sped up? I'd forgotten decorum for a moment, forgotten where I was.

Gods, not now, please don't touch me. Don't say anything. Of all the favors in the world, Gods, just give me this moment. Give me one moment of peace so I can see her again.

The Soturi of Ka Hart spread out, creating an aisle for us to pass through.

The doors to the Seating Room swung open, and my father was announced to Arkasva Batavia. Our party paraded forward, walking down the aisle full of Bamarian Council members. It was a sea of unremarkable faces, of nobles with impressive titles and wealth judging by the shine of their clothing and the size of their jewels. A nobleman my own age stood with an elderly woman wearing head-to-toe silver. He gave me a quick scan, looking me up and down, his lips forming a dismissive sneer when he had finished.

I rolled my eyes. Every nobleman wanted to size me up, particularly those who were recently past their Revelation Ceremony. I walked ahead, my eyes searching for one person. And one person only.

My breath caught.

Lady Lyriana Batavia, Heir to the Arkasva, High Lord of Bamaria, stood beside two other noblewomen, both adorned in golden diadems. They were her older sisters, Lady Meera and Lady Morgana.

There were no windows in the Seating Room, so Lady Lyriana's hair had returned to a dark brown color, a mix between that of her sisters, one of whom had nearly black hair and the other with hair a lighter, ash-like color. They were all wearing the traditional dresses of the south that exposed their shoulders and contained slits in the skirts to accommodate the heat.

I could barely focus on the older heirs. My eyes were on Lady Lyriana, taking in her full appearance, every exquisite detail of her. I could see some of the same features she'd had before—clever, almond-shaped eyes; long black lashes. Her lips had grown full and pouty, her cheekbones high. Her smooth skin was flawless, golden in color from the sun.

I watched her look around the room, her gaze sharp and alert, before my eyes drifted down her body.

My throat tightened.

Her long red gown concealed most of her figure, but the fabric clung to her every curve in a way that made it hard to breathe as we moved closer. A single slit ran from her ankle to her thigh, revealing thick, shapely legs and delicate golden sandals wrapping up to her knee. And she had breasts that were…definitely not what I should have been staring at.

Did she remember me? Had she been too young the last time we'd seen each other? Perhaps I hadn't been memorable to her. Maybe that afternoon hadn't meant anything; she might have simply offered me the lemon cake and scroll to shut me up so she could return to reading in peace.

My stomach sank at the thought. Maybe that was it. And even if it wasn't, what did it matter? She had been only a child then. I had been a child then. An idiot one at that. Now we were heirs on opposite ends of the Empire with lives and destinies in separate countries that weren't likely to intersect again.

But she was watching me and I couldn't breathe. Her eyes followed my progress into the Seating Room, a small smile on her lips, which were—what color was that? Some mix of pink and red that was making me wish I were an artist so I could have come up with the name of that exact shade of pink, painted it. Bottled it.

I had to get my shit together. This was a state affair, and as an Heir to the Arkasva, she was definitely not available. Most likely, she had some engagement contract with one of the pompous, self-inflated nobles standing behind me.

But she was still looking at me, not in an assessing way like I'd been watched so many times before. She wasn't looking down at me either, she didn't pity me, she also didn't appear to be trying to one-up me. She was…interested. Like she remembered me, and it wasn't a terrible memory for her.

Gods, she was so fucking beautiful. So stunning just standing there. It was hard to remember to look elsewhere, to remember where I was, to see anything other than her—her eyes, her smile, her hair—her…just her. Because everything else before me dimmed in comparison.

I returned her gaze, and a blush filled her cheeks, a shy half-smile spreading across her lips. She looked away first, glancing into the audience, at the noblewoman who'd tugged her down the hall. Jules. She was staring at Jules, smiling and blushing... because of me.

Something in my heart swelled, and...my cock twitched as her gaze returned to mine. There was a small sparkle in her eyes, one that seemed to light up her entire face. It was like she was full of light, and she was the only reason I could see anything at all in this room.

And...Fuck. I was hers.

CHAPTER
THREE

"Welcome to Bamaria, Imperator Hart," Arkasva Batavia said jovially.

There was a pounding in my chest, and I turned away, unable to look at Lady Lyriana any longer without breaking into an idiotically obvious grin that everyone in the room would see. I had to bite the inside of my cheek to keep from smiling.

My father coughed beside me, his gaze narrowing from the sides of his gray eyes. Disapproval was clear in his aura, and an underlying threat tinged beneath it. If I embarrassed him now, if I made one misstep that displeased him....

The smile vanished from my face, a small pit forming in my stomach as I returned my full, Heir-Apparent attention back to Arkasva Batavia. Had my father seen me smile? Did he know what had changed my mood? I prayed he hadn't. He hated to see me happy. Laughter annoyed him. Joy infuriated him. Anything that had ever given me pleasure, he'd been sure to destroy.

For once, I was grateful my power was bound, or he'd have read the emotions in my aura in seconds.

I did all I could to watch the Arkasva stepping forward and not gawk at his youngest daughter. I tried to focus on him not her, but it was so hard to pull my attention from Lady Lyriana and the fact that she was standing so close, breathing in the same air as me, hearing the same words I was in that moment.

I took a deep breath, forcing myself to focus on the High Lord before us.

Arkasva Batavia was tall—nearly six feet in height if I had to guess, just inches shorter than me. But those lost inches were made up for by his golden Laurel. He was a lean man, built like a mage, yet even with his slighter frame, he commanded a kind of quiet presence.

My eyes strayed, catching sight of a bare shoulder, luscious brown waves falling across it, leading down to a collarbone that led to—I forced my gaze back onto the Arkasva. He had short black hair and, well, a forgettable face. But he was proud, I could see that much. The small step he'd taken had put his limp on full display, yet his expression never faltered, and his chin remained high.

A crackle of pleasure emanated from the aura beside me. My father loved seeing another man with weakness. But I didn't get the impression of weakness from Arkasva Batavia. He was clearly in command of himself, not hiding his limp, showing it didn't affect him, didn't slow him down. He felt none of the shame my father was placing upon him. What shame would there be in such an injury? He'd survived a rebellion, survived an assassination attempt. If anything, it meant he was strong.

The only real weakness I saw was the lack of golden thread in his Arkasva robes. They were plain black. He ruled Bamaria, nothing more. That meant he was beholden to the Imperator and the Emperor. That made him susceptible to Imperator Kormac stationing his men on the border and inside his country.

My father thanked the Arkasva for the warm welcome, his voice so kind and full of sincerity I felt nauseated listening to it. It was his biggest lie that he had any compassion in him at all, yet over and over again, heads of state and citizens of Glemaria fell for it. They thought him noble, honorable, charming. They didn't see the monster that tormented me or my mother.

"And once more, the young Heir Apparent has honored us with his presence in Bamaria," Arkasva Batavia said, his arms outstretched to me. He offered a wide, genuine, if not warm smile. He didn't seem to be that warm of a man—more practiced at the ways in which an Arkasva was expected to conduct himself—but his words, at least, felt honest. I'd give him that. I'd heard enough lying Arkasvim to know the difference. "Not so young now, though. Congratulations on taking part in your upcoming Revelation Ceremony."

"Thank you, your grace. I am pleased to return to Bamaria once more," I said carefully, hoping my accent hadn't shown.

"We are honored to host you, Lord Rhyan Hart, Heir Apparent to the Arkasva, High Lord of Glemaria, Imperator to the North." He stated my full, formal name and title, but he bowed his chin in respect to my father.

Gods. I hated everything about my title. It was the longest fucking thing in the world to start with; it felt like it took a Gods-damned hour to say. And it wasn't even about me. Nearly every word of it linked me to my father, showed my relationship to him, shouted out to all of Lumeria his complete and total posses-sion of me. Hell, the last half of it was just his title all over again.

But because it was expected of me and I'd already been hit enough today, I pushed my face into the properly humble yet arrogant smile of an Heir Apparent and thanked him for the welcome.

Arkasva Batavia had reached me and my father by now and shook both our hands.

"You must have every noblewoman at home heartsick with looks like this," he said. "And clearly, you'll be a soturion to be feared."

My father laughed at this, the sound full of delight. "I thank you, your grace. The resemblance between us grows stronger each day. And I am quite proud of the man he's becoming."

Arkasva Batavia grinned.

So, I looked like my father when someone else was complimenting me.

Arkasva Batavia then gestured to his daughters, and my heart nearly dropped. Gods. I tried to remember the custom here. Was I about to shake her hand? Touch her?

My palm started to sweat, and I quickly brushed it against my tunic.

"Lady Meera Batavia, Heir Apparent," Arkasva Batavia said proudly. "I'm sure you remember from your previous visit when you were all children. She will be coming into her title and celebrating her Revelation Ceremony next year."

The eldest daughter and Heir Apparent was beautiful in an ethereal way, elegant, and lean in build like her father. She wore a rather simple diadem that shined as she bent into a curtsy, her hands at her sides.

So, no touching. I tried not to show my disappointment.

I nodded and smiled at her as she resumed her position. Lady Morgana was introduced next. Unlike her elder sister, she had a wild, earthy look about her. Her eyes flicked between me and my father before narrowing like she'd seen something she didn't like, before dropping into her own brief curtsy. She'd performed every formality flawlessly, but somehow, from her execution, I'd gotten the feeling she'd just flipped me off.

I couldn't really blame her.

Then I was ushered in front of...*her*. Her eyes widened, and I was close enough to make out the barest hints of gold and green sparkling amongst the brown of her irises. She sucked in a breath, causing her chest to rise. I stared like a fucking idiot.

She curtsied slowly, artfully, with a flourish of her hands at the end as if she'd been dancing. The movement caused her bracelets to chime with the same musical sound I'd heard all those years ago. So, she still liked wearing jingly jewelry.

I bit down on my lip to keep from smiling again. My father was too close, watching me too carefully. Lady Lyriana's eyes settled on me again, and too late, I realized I was still making a ridiculous face.

She looked past me, her cheeks flushed, and I didn't need to turn to know she was looking once more at Jules.

I wanted to reach out and assure her I liked the way her jewelry sounded, a lot. That I liked…everything about her. But it was against protocol, and my father was too near. I clenched my fists at my sides.

Arkasva Batavia ushered us to the other side of his Seat before he sat, and I was forced to stand there for what felt like an eternity as we were greeted by the Bamarian Council, an endless round of self-important noblemen and women. The entire time, I was stared at by nobles, glared at by my father, and trying desperately and failing to not watch every one of Lady Lyriana's movements—every shift of her weight between her feet, every sigh, every slight stretch that exposed her thigh or the arch of her neck.

When I'd nodded at my final Bamarian noble, Arkasva Batavia clapped his hands.

"Now that you have been welcomed by Bamaria, it's time we showed you one of Bamaria's greatest treasures."

I stifled a groan. It was tradition for the host Arkasva to take a visiting Arkasva somewhere to show off, but myself to fucking Moriel, I was exhausted. And I wasn't sure how much longer I could stand to be in public.

"Wonderful," my father said, sounding excited. Even his aura felt light. But there was a hint of annoyance I easily recognized. He was a good liar. "The last time we visited, you chose to take us on a tour of the Katurium."

"Yes. Well, we must, of course, allow one the Empire's

greatest soturi to see where we do our warrior training. But this time, I thought we'd try something new. We'll be taking a private tour of the Great Library. Bamaria houses the largest collection of scrolls in the Lumerian Empire. We have seraphim waiting outside the fortress, ready to take you there."

With that, we were dismissed. Lady Lyriana broke protocol first, grabbing Jules's hand and racing from the room the same way she'd come. Fuck. I could swear the room dimmed upon her exit.

Lady Meera and Lady Morgana devolved into an intense conversation as they exited the Seating Room next. Meera walked a bit slower, waving to and greeting each person she saw, while Morgana appeared impatient.

I was escorted back outside into the sweltering southern heat and boarded onto a seraphim alone with my personal guards behind a partition. Exhaustion from wearing my public face for so long under so much scrutiny had me laying back, my eyes shutting the moment we were airborne, though I had marveled at finally being able to stare out an open window.

I jolted back awake as our seraphim touched down, the floor of the carriage shifting as the bird settled onto the ground. Outside was a long expanse of desert sand. Scholar's Harbor. Three pyramids built of golden brick loomed before me. They were all different sizes, and I knew each housed a different type of title. They'd been built at different times, each one growing in size to accommodate the ever-increasing collection of written works that had been produced since the Drowning.

I stepped outside, surrounded by my guard, walking past two dark-skinned and incredibly tall soturi, each holding a sword to guard the smallest of the libraries.

I had always wanted to visit the Great Library of Bamaria. But in truth, my feet were carrying me forward purely from a desire to see Lady Lyriana again, to be back in her presence. And maybe getting out of the heat was also a factor. The sun seemed to beat more harshly here. Luckily, the air was markedly cooler inside the pyramid, and just beyond the entrance we were greeted by the head librarian and each handed amethyst lamps to carry forward, but I couldn't focus. Lady Lyriana was so close.

"I don't know, Jules," she said at one point. "But maybe? I think so."

I wasn't sure what she was talking about, but I was excited to hear her voice. It was just as beautiful as the rest of her.

The librarian gave a short history of the library, which had been built right after the Drowning and had filled so quickly with scrolls that had been saved or found preserved in the ocean, the second pyramid had to be built.

I tried to focus on her words. I did. But I couldn't take my eyes or attention off Lady Lyriana.

When we were admitted inside and separated into small tour groups, I, somehow, by sheer luck, ended up in hers.

She grinned at me. "Your grace, Lord Rhyan. It's very nice to see you again."

We were led forward by our librarian. Lady Julianna was in our group as well, plus all our escorts.

"And you as well, your grace." I forgot to say her name; I was so busy puzzling out whether she'd meant her words or was simply offering a formal greeting. She knew I'd visited before, and so we'd met. But did she remember the library and the cake? We were in a library now. If she remembered, this was the time to mention it.

My heart pounded.

She frowned, and I felt like a fucking idiot. I needed to say more, to do more. But what?

"And you, Lady Julianna," I said, turning to her cousin.

She smiled brightly then shared a look with Lady Lyriana that I couldn't read.

About me? Good? Bad? Fuck.

We walked through the various levels of the pyramid,

passing shelves and shelves of scrolls, as we were told about the different sections. Our tour guide talked non-stop, but quickly her lecture became an ongoing conversation between him and Lady Lyriana. By the third level, Lyriana herself had taken over the tour. She spun on her heels gesturing at the shelves and grabbing random scrolls that our tour guide kept snatching back from her to return, trying and failing to hide his annoyance.

But now that she was the leader, I found I was finally able to pay attention. I was fascinated by her description of the under-pyramid below ground full of restricted scrolls and levels for repair. She pointed out which scrolls were copies and which were originals that had come from Lumeria Matavia. She seemed to be an expert in how much damage each scroll contained.

The way her eyes lit up as she found another scroll to discuss and the excitement in her voice as we moved through every level was intoxicating. And adorable. She was so elegant, so beautiful to watch, so full of passion for knowledge. Every twirl of her wrist as she grabbed another scroll caused her bracelets to jingle. I had to hide my smiles and nearly walked into a shelf once, fixated on the way she stood on her toes to grab a scroll from a shelf above her head.

"What do you think, Lord Rhyan?" she asked as we neared the end, almost back at our starting point.

Our tour guide looked glum-faced and shot daggers from his eyes at her, which Lady Julianna quickly noted. With a shake of her head, the tour guide cleared his expression.

"I'm quite impressed. You're a natural in the library. You could be a librarian yourself," I said.

Lady Lyriana nodded, an expression I couldn't read flitting over her face. "I suppose."

"I remember visiting a much smaller library the last time I was here." My heart pounded. Did she remember? Did she remember me?

She looked thoughtful, something playful and mischievous in her eyes. "This is the smallest library of the three."

I narrowed my gaze. Was she playing with me? "No others in Bamaria come any smaller?"

A small smile spread across her lips. "Most are interested in bigger."

I coughed. "I'm not most." I still had no answer to my question or any idea what she was thinking. I could have sworn she was flirting with me, but she seemed guarded. Which made sense. We were, after all, surrounded by escorts, librarians, and the other nobles on this tour.

Including my Godsdamned father, whom I found watching me from a few feet away. Fucking hell. I straightened my posture and removed any semblance of enjoyment from my face. I already knew how ridiculous he'd think this excursion was—and what a waste of time. It was better I didn't anger him anymore today if it could be helped.

His eyebrows narrowed at me, and my entire body tensed, but then he started up a conversation with the head librarian, his face full of false delight and interest.

Lady Lyriana had retreated several feet from me, her arm linked with Lady Julianna's as they whispered something I could not hear.

I didn't want to come across to her any stranger than I already had and turned away, only to find an Afeya in the Great Library.

I stumbled back. My stomach twisted. Afeya looked Lumerian, human enough, but they were immortals who shape-shifted their appearances at will, changing the color of their skin and hair. Some even took the form of animals, fully and partially, though they rarely did so outside their own lands. Since Afeya could not perform any magic of their own free will, the most basic form of trickery they engaged in was getting a Lumerian to request they have access to their powers of glamour. But most of their magic involved something far more sinister and dangerous.

This Afeya had long dark hair and a mix of masculine and feminine features, but wore what was undoubtedly a masculine body. His skin was pale blue in color, dark whorls tattooed across his arms and legs with diamonds in the center. His eyes were completely focused on Lady Lyriana.

A feline smile crossed his lips as his gaze shifted to me. Eyes of pure violet. My stomach was in knots, my body crawling with the feeling of having become prey to this predator. I stared down, afraid to meet his gaze.

You can look away, my young lord, but we shall meet soon. You're not the heir I seek.

A smooth musical voice spoke the words in my mind. My own thoughts playing tricks on me? Or was it…the Afeya? My heart pounded. I looked up again, and he was gone. But his aura seemed to linger as something still shivered inside of me.

"Lord Rhyan," someone yelled. "Your grace?"

It took me a moment to hear their voice. I seemed to be lost in a fog from the Afeya's presence.

When I registered the shout, I whirled around, yelling back, "What!"

I stared at Lady Lyriana, whose mouth fell open at my outburst.

"Apologies, your grace," I said quickly. "I didn't hear you."

"Um," she said, looking uneasy, "we're going back to Cresthaven now."

I nodded. "Thank you." I strolled past her before I could embarrass myself further, trying to shake the strange feeling of the Afeya watching me, watching Lady Lyriana. What was he doing here? What did he want? Was this normal? Did Arkasva Batavia know an Afeya was visiting his land? Watching his youngest daughter?

I closed my eyes, still seeing his face, still sensing his presence, his voice, and then, just like that, the sensation was gone, and we were escorted back out into the sun to our carriages.

The moment my seraphim landed, I was escorted straight to the guest wing with my father.

I was given my own private suite, an expansive rounded room that reminded me of the library in the heir's wing but with a single shelf full of scrolls and an opened balcony. Despite the heat outside, cool air gushed through the room in refreshing waves. Clear pipes outlined the windows with water rushing through them, catching the light of the sun. Rainbows danced inside of the glass. The wealthy homes and fortresses in the south all had built-in cooling towers, as well as waterways that left the indoors in moderate temperatures for the summer. If only we could install them on the litter for our journey home.

I wasn't going to think about that now. Or anything. I was exhausted. I'd spent too much time with my father. Too much time socializing. I was done after making such a prolonged public appearance, and from overthinking every word and interaction between me and Lyriana.

I needed to relax and had one goal in mind for how to do so. I undid my belt, slid off my boots and socks, tossed off my tunic, and sank onto the cool bed in nothing but the shortpants I wore beneath.

It was my first moment of peace in weeks, and I had every intention of taking advantage of it alone, in private. As well as using it to relieve some freshly built tension from the last few hours.

I exhaled slowly, my hand sliding down my stomach to the waistband of my pants, which were already stretching to full capacity. I was so fucking ready. Ready to forget the past few weeks. To forget everything. To feel good. To imagine her.

But my door slammed open, and I sat up with a growl.

"Comfortable?" My father loomed in the doorway.

My personal escort was situated outside the door, so I was

meant to have privacy. Soturion Bowen had been *protecting* me since I could walk, but he only offered me around a quarter of his loyalty. He'd been the soturion who'd let me escape all those years ago to find the library and Lady Lyriana. And he'd been the one to call me back. Of course, it had taken him hours to find me, and I wasn't exactly hiding that well. So, I had to give him that. And should I come across any enemy who meant me harm, he would defend me with his life.

But should I come across my father? I barely saw the point of Bowen's existence. Especially since today was apparently one of those days when he was exhibiting his three quarters' loyalty directly to his Imperator.

I stumbled from the bed to my feet, trying not to focus on my near-nakedness, or the bruises in various degrees of healing and color across my torso. "Your highness. What can I do for you?"

"Put some Godsdamned clothes on to start." He slammed the door behind him and stalked toward me, his hand resting on the hilt of his sword. His gray eyes zeroed in on my ribcage, and his gaze traced the wounds on my skin with every step he took.

I squeezed my eyes shut, my stomach twisting and dick softening. Could I not have a fucking moment to myself?

"I apologize, your highness. After the long journey and tour, I wanted to bathe before our formal dinner with the Arkasva and Council."

"You wanted to jerk off," he snarled. He folded his arms across his chest and laughed. "Which one got you worked up? Eldest? Middle? Youngest?" He cocked his head to the side, a knowing gleam in his gray eyes as a grin slid snake-like across his face. "Youngest."

I glared. "I could barely tell them apart."

"Oh, but I think you could. She was in your little library tour group, after all. And even if she wasn't, she stands out, doesn't she? You've got an eye on her. The youngest one. I remember now, that was the one you fixated on the last time, always trying to sneak into her wing, follow her around and play. Still intact, I bet. Lyriana. Pretty name. Pretty girl." The threat in his voice was evident.

My hands clenched at my sides. "Did you really come in here to discuss with me which heir I found attractive?"

"I came to discuss which girl you'd like to fuck."

I snarled. "How is that any of your business?"

"Whichever girl you fuck will always be my business. My grandchild's beginning lives inside your Godsdamned cock right now." His eyes flicked down to my shortpants. "If you ever get it back up. So, yes. I did come here for that."

"You never cared at home."

"State business is my business."

"Aren't the Glemarian girls I *fuck* also state business?"

He chuckled. "Only if you're sloppy." His eyes narrowed. "Lady Meera is out of the question. For the record. She'll be Arkasva Batavia soon—there's a reason Heir Apparents do not court each other. He'll have her married to the most powerful Ka in Bamaria. Probably those silver wretches. Ka Grey. Lady Morgana...perhaps?" He shrugged his shoulders. "She's not to my taste. But still, she'd be best used to make a profitable alliance for her father with another country in the south. She'd be a good way to appease Ka Kormac in their overreach. At least, that's what I would do were I in her father's position. I heard the Bastardmaker has lost his wife again."

My nostrils flared. The way he talked about women—like they were just things to be bartered and sold for profit, moved around to advance the deals of the arkasvim rather than people who had thoughts and feelings and desires—it was exactly how he treated Mother. Like a thing. A thing he hated.

It was how he treated me.

"I thank you for the lesson in politics, your highness," I said, hoping to end the conversation.

"But Lyriana," he said, stroking his chin.

"Lady Lyriana," I growled before I could help myself, my accent thick.

My father clucked his tongue in disapproval at my tone. "*Lady Lyriana*," he mocked. "She's the true spare. Third in line to a coveted seat. Worthless. Never going to be Heir Apparent. Not needed to secure much in here. She could waste her time sitting on the Council. But for what purpose? Now, she...she could fetch a pretty price."

"Last time I checked, heirs were not for sale."

"Everything and everyone is always for sale. You just need to find the right price point. Or pain point, as it were." He continued stroking his chin. "Now, if her father wanted to make some friends in the north, some powerful friends, like, say, an Imperator—one who was currently not holding his country captive...."

So Ka Kormac's presence at the border was more sinister than I'd realized. It all began to make sense—why this visit, why now. My father was here to observe, to learn. It wasn't enough for him to rule half the Empire, to have full and complete power over Glemaria and full jurisdiction across the north. He was looking to expand. My bet...Hartavia, his true home, was his target. It would be his little way of making himself feel legitimate as a ruler and one-upping Imperator Kormac—his rival and the only man who held more power than him beside the Emperor. The Imperator to the south was the Emperor's nephew.

"You like her?" he asked me, his voice suddenly conversational, like we were friends.

"Who?" I asked innocently. "You've mentioned quite a few girls in the past minute."

"You know which one, idiot. The fire-head. The one who's such a spare, she could afford to be late to our greeting ceremony."

"I don't even know her."

"I'll believe you when you say that without making fists.

And while you're trying to convince me, go ahead and unclench that jaw of yours. Always your tell."

I breathed out and softened my hands at my side. "I'm speaking the truth. I don't know her. You already know this."

"But you wouldn't be, say, upset if you were forced to see her on a regular basis?"

I was stepping into a trap. I was sure of it. "Last I checked, no one likes being forced into anything, your highness."

He chuckled. "I'll need you to secure things for me up north, not begin a courtship with a southern heir. Especially a southern spare. Remember that well. So when I leave this room, I want you to sit back, grab your cock, and get her tits out of your fucking system. But perhaps in a year's time, you may be able to have her. Arkturion Kane needs a new wife."

"Arkturion Kane!"

"Rhyan," he clucked his tongue. "Rhyan, Rhyan, my boy." He stepped forward. "You forgot to say, *your highness*."

And with that, he clocked me in the jaw.

"Do you want another?"

I rubbed at the tender skin, hoping I had enough sunleaves with me to treat it and keep a bruise from forming.

"No. Thank you, your highness."

His gray eyes narrowed. "I've never seen you like this before. Except when you get self-righteous over your mother. As if she isn't the most well-treated, wealthiest woman to live in Glemaria." He sneered. "The luxury and ease of life I provide. The sacrifices I've made. And it's never enough for her. Or you."

I remained still, not daring to move, not daring to speak.

"You see, if I ally with the Arkasva of Bamaria, he gains a powerful friend to keep Ka Kormac back," he said, easily switching to a conversational tone with me—as if nothing had happened.

I frowned, eyeing him carefully. "True, your highness. But what do you get from such an arrangement?"

He laughed. "You must really like her. That, or you're dying to see if the hair on her cunt also turns to fire in the sun."

Moriel fucking bastard. What kind of sick fuck said things like that about a girl young enough to be his daughter?

He grinned like he knew he'd struck a chord. "You do, don't you? You've never shown a quarter of this emotion with any girl back home. Believe it or not, Lady Lyriana is more valuable to me than just a way to hold you in check. And I'll be generous with her. Once Kane has put a baby in her belly and her tits swell to twice their size, maybe I'll have a go. And when I'm done... you can lick my cum off her tits and do what you like." With that, he left the room.

I waited to hear the lock click into place before I stomped outside, smashed my fist into the balcony, and roared. Fucking bastard!

He was bluffing. He had to be. Arkasva Batavia would never send his youngest daughter to the other end of the Empire to marry a monster like Arkturion Kane. She'd never be seen again, and other than some fucking lemons being traded, Bamaria had little to do with our country. It didn't make any sense. My father did not hold power over Arkasva Batavia or his half of the Empire.

Except...Bamaria was clearly being occupied by a rogue Imperator. And it wasn't as if the Arkasva could appeal to the power beyond him. The Emperor was the only one with greater authority, and he was Imperator Kormac's uncle, corrupt and willing to take Ka Kormac's side at nearly every turn. Appealing to a higher power was out of the question.

So how else could Arkasva Batavia rid his country of an invading soturi without bringing war to his people? He'd need to be allies with another Imperator. And marrying a daughter to a country's arkturion—that was no small feat. It was almost as prestigious as marrying an arkasva. The logic, I hated to admit it, was there.

Still, what was in it for my father? What value could Lady Lyriana have to him?

None. She was…she was special to me. But my father? He could just as easily make this bargain with Lady Morgana, with Lady Julianna even. And I was sure there was another cousin—even older women of Ka Batavia who were husbandless. If his eyes were set on Lady Lyriana, there was only one reason I could think of, and it was just insane enough to fit him perfectly.

He knew I liked her. Knew it would upset me. Knew he could throw it in my face. Knew she'd be another way for him to control me. Bowen must have told him everything about that afternoon all those years ago. My father had probably been looking for the smallest show of interest or affection today. He now had all of my interactions with Lady Lyriana in the Bamarian Court and at the library to sift through. And I wasn't sure how well I'd played my hand back there. I'd been taken so aback, I'd been so enchanted….

But I needed to convince him otherwise—that I had no concern for her at all. That I felt no affection, no attraction, nothing. Which meant I had to stay away from Lady Lyriana, ignore her, forget her. My stomach twisted. For a moment, she'd been a bright light in a fucking horrible year. Years. But I could give that up.

I was hers, but she wasn't mine, and she never would be.

I had to do this. To keep her safe, I *would* do this.

I finally did take that bath, followed by a brief nap. Refreshed, I processed my father's threat again with a clearer head. Though my father considered Imperator Kormac his rival, he'd never make a move against him. If war broke out between Ka Kormac and Ka Hart, the Emperor's army would turn against us. We'd be able to wait out several weeks or even months of a siege in the mountains. But in the end, in open battle, we wouldn't stand a chance—and he knew that.

Would Arkasva Batavia know that sending Lady Lyriana to

the north would be an empty promise? Would he realize such an arrangement would do nothing to improve his position, or hold back Imperator Kormac's forces?

I had to believe that he did, though I was still determined to ignore her and throw my father off her scent.

Still, one final possibility weighed heavily on me. Taking Lady Lyriana away from Bamaria wouldn't strengthen the country, it would weaken it. One less heir to Ka Batavia—the bloodline that had ruled for a thousand years. With the power and magic flowing through the country, that would be tempting for other rulers.

The women of Ka Batavia had remained in power for a thousand years by passing the Seat only to each other and marrying only inside of Bamaria. Only one person could put a stop to that and order a marriage to take place with a foreign Ka. With a foreign warlord.

Imperator Kormac. But he wasn't in Bamaria now. Only his wolves.

I took small comfort in that fact as I was escorted to dinner downstairs.

The room was full of Bamarian nobles, members of the Council, and their personal guards. But the walls weren't only lined with the Soturi of Ka Batavia in golden armor. Silver armor peppered the crowd.

A wolfish aura prodded at me, the sensation dark, and predatory.

Shit. Standing in the center of the dining hall was the only other man as sinister and evil as my sire. The one man that could in fact order Lady Lyriana to marry a monster like Arkturion Kane.

Arkasva Kormac, High Lord of Korteria, Imperator to the South.

FOUR

The southern Imperator seemed to be the opposite of my father in nearly every way. He had blonde hair he wore loose to his shoulders, tanned skin, and nearly black eyes. Everything about his appearance was striking and perfectly polished. His aura announced his power, his control, his viciousness. There was no question as to who the Imperator was, what he stood for, or what side you were on with him.

My father wasn't unpolished, but he appeared rather gruff in comparison, like a veteran warrior just home from battle, one of the men. He gave the illusion he was someone that the everyday Lumerian could relate to, someone who understood their plight, nothing more than the common soturion acting as Arkasva and Imperator. He saved the bite of his aura for me, for his enemies, for my mother. In public, he convinced everyone he was a sweet, amicable ruler.

He couldn't be more deadly or cruel, but he hid it well. Imperator Kormac was more upfront.

He stalked toward me and my father.

"Devon! If I'd known how prompt you'd be in your arrival, I'd have come sooner."

"Good to see you, Avery!" my father shouted happily. "Only because we agreed to meet here instead of Korteria."

So they had agreed to meet in advance. My father had kept this detail from me. This couldn't all be coincidence. Sure, they met all the time, but in the capitol, in Numeria. Or Imperator Kormac came to the north. What in Lumeria were they up to?

"This is where the action is, after all," Imperator Kormac said. He stepped back, offering me a wolfish grin, his black eyes running greedily up and down my body. Something withered inside of me. His eyes, the way he watched me, the presumption in them, it reminded me of—

I wiped my hand on my tunic. No. Not thinking about that.

A larger man in a red arkturion cloak joined his side—Waryn Kormac, the southern Imperator's brother, otherwise known as the Bastardmaker.

"Your grace," Imperator Kormac said. "Do I have this right? You'll be participating in the Revelation Ceremony this year?"

I glanced at my father, whose nostrils flared with such fury that I turned back to Imperator Kormac.

"Yes, your highness," I said. "I will be unbound at the end of summer." Not illegally on my birthday this past winter. I was certainly not already in possession of a vorakh that I'd been forced to conceal by my father. Definitely not itching this very moment with power barely contained beneath my skin.

"Path?" he asked.

"Soturion, of course."

He shared a look with his brother before his gaze roamed to my feet and back up again. "We'll be glad to have you in the fight. We need more men. Akadim are running rampant. And though the Soturion Academy down here insists on women becoming soturi, I think we both know it's men who stop the beasts. Not the ones who join the fight and leave the moment a baby's in their belly."

I stiffened. My mother had been a soturion and kept from fighting the moment my father realized she was carrying me.

"If akadim are running rampant," I said, "we must need all the help we can get."

Imperator Kormac laughed. "You have the makings of a politician. I'll give you that. Did you teach him to be this clever, Devon?"

My father chuckled. "Taught him everything he knows and damn proud."

I grimaced.

Imperator Kormac narrowed his eyes, suddenly sizing me up. "Were it not for how potent the land here made magic, and its close location, I'd have my men attending the Glemarian Academy." He laughed. "How are you enjoying this fine country, your grace?"

"It's hot," I said, simply.

"Yes. Too hot. Forces women to wear less clothes. Something I always appreciate. Have you gotten your fill yet of the arkasva's daughters?" he leered.

"He has his eye on one," my father said with a knowing look.

"Don't we all." Imperator Kormac grinned wickedly and my stomach sank. They were talking about Lyriana.

A herald announced the appearance of Arkasva Batavia and his daughters in that moment.

My father's head snapped toward me at once. I frowned and inspected my fingernails for dirt. If he was waiting to see my reaction to Lady Lyriana, he'd be waiting all night. Especially if a second Imperator was observing. But that second Imperator looked disinterested in further discussion and headed off to the corner where his warlord had retreated.

Some lesser members of the Council entered the dining hall. That nobleman I'd seen earlier, with the gryphon-shit-eating grin on his face, had returned along with the ancient woman who'd apparently never met a piece of silver jewelry she didn't like.

Seriously, did she think the pieces would disappear if she didn't wear every last one?

The nobleman found me the moment he entered the room, his eyes flicking up and down my body in disdain as he guided the ancient woman to the table. An elderly man with a silver sash around his blue tunic strolled behind them, seemingly unaware of where he was.

I exhaled sharply, mentally regurgitating the names of the noble Kavim I'd memorized as a boy. If this pompous ass was going to spend his time looking at me like that, I might as well know his name. His grandmother—I assumed that was how the elder woman was related to him—had greeted me earlier and been introduced, but so had a dozen nobles, and I'd maybe been distracted by another noblewoman, who liked lemon cake, instead of remembering which names belonged to which faces.

There was Ka Shavo—they were the shadows and spies. Their lady had only shown her face but no body when I'd met her. Ka Scholar were all back at the Great Library, far more interested in scrolls than silver and politics. Ka Elys loved to showcase their sigil and were known to wear orange or purple exclusively to announce if they were from the Bamarian or Elyrian branch. They all had a similar look that this noble did not have at all.

He rested his hand on his silver belt, and an oversized silver sigil ring flared out beneath the torches overhead.

Ah, Ka Grey. Right. Which made him...Lord Tristan. Little fucker. I knew his type. Bound to come over to me the moment protocol allowed so he could verbally size me up, prove to himself that he was more worthy than the Heir Apparent up north, by stumping me on some obscure Bamarian fact I'd never need to know so he could...I didn't know. Jerk himself off at night knowing he was important? They all did the same thing.

He was probably fuming that his grandparents, as head of their Ka, had greeted me earlier, and he'd been left in his seat.

I knew I had his attention but turned mine back to the parade of Council and family members joining the party in advance of the Arkasva. Next came Lady Arianna—the younger sister to the Lady Arkasva Batavia, Lady Lyriana's mother. Lady Arianna had slightly faded red hair and was undeniably beautiful. She'd been extremely poised when she'd greeted me earlier. Two noblewomen of Ka Batavia followed on either side of her, carrying themselves with all the markings of heirs—minus the diadems. One I recognized right away as Jules.

Lady Arianna had been next to the Seat before Arkasva Batavia had taken power. If I recalled, the rebellion that had earned him his limp had been fought in her name, though at the time she'd had no idea. Allegedly. I assumed the other girl beside her was her daughter. They had the same sort of look to them, though none of the same physical features.

I could see the Batavia traits in Arianna—the reddish hair, the high cheekbones, and the pouty lips that reminded me of Lady Lyriana. But the girl, she was skinny and sulky and looked completely miserable. Her blonde hair had been curled and braided across her forehead, styled to look like some sort of self-made diadem. A bit desperate. And disrespectful, at least as far as court politics went.

My mother had once had a rival who'd taken to wearing a headband so far forward that it often fell across her forehead, becoming a false diadem. My mother had been furious at this, screaming about it after formal functions, venting to me in private. Of course, my father didn't care about the slight one bit. He'd been fucking Mother's rival.

Arkturion Aemon entered the dining hall next. Known as the deadliest warrior in Lumeria, he'd earned the nickname of the Ready after he was said to have single-handedly quashed the Ka Kasmar rebellion. Tales of his strength, heroism, and violence entertained a lot of soturi back home though not in my father's court. There, the only arkturion worthy of praise was Arkturion

Kane. Personally, I couldn't think of a single thing praiseworthy about the scum other than that he could sing some old nursery rhyme about vorakh by belching. A rare talent, indeed. He'd risen to his ranks not because of his fighting prowess but because of his taste for brutality and a special ability to kiss my father's ass. He was a beast, a poor excuse of a man not suitable for Lady Lyriana. Not suitable for any woman, for that matter.

My hands clenched again at the idea of my father bringing Lady Lyriana to Glemaria, of giving her to that.... And yet, the southern Imperator was here, clearly colluding with my father. One handshake, and Imperator Kormac could very well order Lady Lyriana to Arkturion Kane's wedding bed.

Over my dead body.

The Ready's observant eyes fell on me, pulling me from my thoughts. His lips quirked up as if he'd found something to approve of in me, then his attention swiveled to my father and the other Imperator. The Ready sneered and gave a curt nod, his aura casting itself out in one powerful stroke as he made his way to stand against the wall, creating a space into which Arkasva Batavia and his heirs could enter at last.

The eldest, Lady Meera, arrived first, then the second daughter, Lady Morgana, and then Lyriana stood in the doorway. *Lady* Lyriana. I hadn't been given permission yet to drop her title or use the nickname the other girls used. But I wanted to use it. I wanted to have the honor of calling her that, of being on a casual-name basis.

She stepped all the way in, wearing the same gown from earlier, but now she'd adorned her arms with additional golden cuffs and replaced her earlier necklace with a larger one, perhaps to make her look more formal for dinner. That slit on her dress revealed the silky golden skin of her leg. The sudden need to go to her, to talk to her, crashed over me like a wave.

Then I remembered. I could not show any interest or give her any attention at all.

I thought when my father had announced his plans to use the blade on me, it had meant he'd thought his old techniques of torturing me were failing. I barely responded to his hits and punches anymore. I'd become too practiced at turning off my thoughts, at running so deep into my mind I barely registered the pain of his whip. He'd caught on. His old punishments had ceased to satisfy him. So he'd taken to hurting my mother in front of me, and much as it killed me, I'd learned to fall silent then, too, to keep my face still as he dragged her across the floor, and then as he did Gods knew what to her behind closed doors while I was forced to listen. The more I fought back, the more I defended her, the more pain he inflicted. My mother had begged me to stop intervening, insisted I was making things worse.

Perhaps even that was becoming less enjoyable to my father. He didn't just want a human punching bag to relieve his anger. It was more sinister than that. He enjoyed seeing the effect of his power on others, observing the pain that he created and knowing it was his doing.

Lady Lyriana would be like a fun new toy for him—on every level.

This was why it was better not to feel. Caring was dangerous. Opening my heart, perilous. I'd been lost in a fantasy earlier. It'd been a temporary moment of delusion brought about by Lady Lyriana's beauty, the way she'd seemed to own the Great Library. The memory of a girl who'd let me sit in peace beside her for hours without question, offering me my first hint of friendship while we co-read the same scroll and shared lemon cake.

Shifting myself back behind my father and escort, I'd hoped to be seated at the table as far away from her as possible, some-where where I'd be able to focus and concentrate. I'd keep my eyes off her and keep my father from toying with this absurd idea any longer.

"Your grace." The Ready approached me.

"Arkturion Aemon," I said. "It's an honor to see you again." I'd met him briefly at my last visit but only from afar. Generally, warlords didn't spend much time with children. He'd been the only member of the Bamarian Council missing when we'd arrived.

"Ah, you remember. You've grown! But you were easily recognizable to me. Come. You've been around old men long enough. I'll seat you with the youths of Bamaria. You can enjoy your dinner."

I swallowed, my throat dry, suspecting my father would disapprove, but he nodded and waved me off as if this had been his idea.

"You'll be a soturion this fall?" asked the Ready.

I nodded. "Yes. At the Soturion Academy in Glemaria."

"Brutal school."

"It does its job," I said neutrally. "We have more akadim up north, so the threat is rather motivating."

The monsters of the old world hated sunlight and heat. They thrived in the north where the days were shorter, the sun wasn't as bright most of the year, and the winter came early and left late. It was a veritable playground for them.

The beasts were a problem everywhere, including beyond the Lumerian borders in the lands of humans—those who had not been born of Lumeria. Most Lumerians of the north became soturi and were deployed to the Empire's border and beyond, attempting to stymy the akadims' numbers. But every year, the akadim persisted, taking our soldiers down if they were lucky. The unlucky ones were turned, becoming akadim themselves— overgrown, soul-sucking, heartless monsters.

The Ready nodded. "I've been hearing reports. I'm thankful to the north for keeping them at bay. We have our own issues down here." His eyes flickered to Imperator Kormac, an aura full of darkness and anger pushing from his body before he pulled it back, resuming a calm face. "Well, I'm sure you're looking forward to your studies. If you're anything like I've heard about the bloodline of your Ka, you will make Glemaria very proud."

Just what I'd always wanted. Right now, I'd have settled just for being able to pick up a sword without my bound strength itching to the point of torture inside me.

The Ready turned at a table and stopped. "Here we are, your grace." He gestured to an open seat.

Right beside Lady Lyriana.

"Your grace," she said quietly. "Lord Rhyan."

I jerked my chin in response, shoved out my chair, and fell into it, leaning back and scowling. I felt her stiffen beside me as I ignored her completely. Fuck!

"Lord Rhyan Hart," said a smooth, polished voice. Lord Grey.

I waited a beat, donning my most bored Heir Apparent look before finally glancing up at the Ka Grey boy sitting across from me.

"Sorry. Did you mean to address me?" I asked. "Or were you simply thinking of me and unable to help yourself from calling out my name? Because I have to say, my lord, I'm flattered. But overly polished rich boys like yourself aren't really my type."

Deep brown eyes assessed me as Lord Tristan Grey cocked his head to the side. His aura flared. Oh, he was definitely pissed. So fucking easily.

"Well?" I asked, drumming my fingers against the table. "If you truly meant to earn my attention, you're missing a rather large portion of my title."

My Godsdamned fucking title. I hated it, but I was also just enough of an asshole that I wasn't above throwing it in the faces of snotty lords who looked ready to try me.

"I wasn't sure if you were asleep, your grace. I wasn't sure you heard Lady Lyriana greet you. My apologies," Lord Tristan said evenly. His gaze flicked beside me as he offered a smile that even I knew was charming to Lyriana.

I glanced over just enough to see her smiling back, genuine gratitude in her expression. Beautiful. And so rare in Heirs to the Arkasva. She certainly knew how to put on a public game face, but she seemed to drop it more often than any other noble I'd seen in courts across the Empire. I could see the training drilled into her—her perfect posture, the slight tilts of her head, the polite smile—and yet, the girl from the library was still there. Defiant. Wild. Accepting. Sweet. The passion for knowledge she had, the excitement for reading she'd shown at the Great Library —she'd dropped her mask then.

Then it hit me. She hadn't dropped her mask for me, but for books. And now for Tristan. For Lord fucking Grey.

He had been coming to her defense, allowing her to save face after my slight. He may have been sizing me up earlier, but I'd offended Lady Lyriana the moment I'd sat down at the table, possibly the moment I'd stepped foot in Cresthaven. I was the asshole who'd been rude since I'd arrived. I was the fucking villain here. All because of my father's threat.

What I wouldn't have given to wipe that smug grin off his face or smack the obvious interest from his eyes as he watched her. Perhaps they'd be married. A future lord of his Ka and a Bamarian Council member, he was definitely a fitting match for an heir. Though, from what I remembered, Ka Grey was the wealthiest Ka in Bamaria thanks to their silver mining. He'd actually be a smarter match for Lady Meera.

Myself to Moriel. My father really had gotten to me if I was sitting here playing Bamarian matchmaker. Gods.

"Well then, your grace, what is your type?" Jules asked, her voice bright and teasing like we were old friends.

I leaned forward, looking past Lady Lyriana to her cousin. "Maybe it's you, Lady Julianna," I said with a wink.

She burst into laughter. "Nice try, your grace." There was something so warm and friendly about her. It was a shame I had to play the asshole for my remaining visit. I could see her being a friend. Perhaps that was why Lady Lyriana was so close to her.

I leaned over, took her hand in mine. "Do I look like a liar?"

"You look like you were born a noble, and all nobles are liars." Lady Lyriana watched me, her hazel eyes golden with light.

"And how would you know I'm not the exception?"

"Because I know you," she said, still teasing, and yet those words…they felt like a weight on me. Like there was so much more to what she meant.

I swallowed, unable to find the words to respond. The whole table around us seemed to go silent, watching the stand-off between us. I released Jules's hand and sat back, folded my arms across my chest. My heart pounded beneath them.

Lady Lyriana looked at me even after I'd turned away. I could feel it, her eyes, her energy, even without an aura present. Before I could help myself, I turned back toward her, took her in fully for the first time since being seated beside her. My breath nearly caught as I saw her up close. Her long waves had been curled and threaded with tiny golden beads. I could better see the details of her new necklace; it looked like it had been made of golden seraphim feathers.

"Well then, your grace," I said, not trusting myself to say her name out loud without giving myself away, "if all nobles are liars, and you are noble, tell me, what is your latest lie?"

"That this is real," she said. And she smiled at me. Gods, she was so beautiful when she smiled, even if it was a smile laced with anger and vitriol, even when she'd just told me to my face her smile was a lie. I had a feeling she'd look beautiful wearing any expression.

Arkasva Batavia called the dinner to order. Water dancers moved into the center of the room, their bodies undulating in perfectly synchronized movements as drums beat around the room, and over a dozen musicians picked up instruments. Every single set of eyes moved to the dancers. Except for one.

My father's. He was watching me and Lady Lyriana.

I focused on the water dancers, doing all I could to maintain a neutral face as Lord Grey began asking Lyriana about her recent dance performances.

"Are you a fan of water dancing?" Lord Grey asked, turning his attention back on me. "Bamaria is famous for its dancers."

"I can appreciate anything that requires talent."

My eyes flicked to Lady Lyriana, dying to see her dance. I already knew she'd be amazing from the way she moved her body with such subtle grace and control.

"Tell us, your grace, what is your talent?" he asked.

"I'll show you mine if you show me yours."

"A clever deflection," he said smoothly.

"Or I'm not in the business of throwing what I believe to be talent in the face of others upon first meeting. But, since you have inquired and shown yours with precision, I recently wanted to perfect the art of being a pompous ass. Any tips?" I asked.

Lord Grey sneered, his neck reddening with color, his head cocked to the side.

"Did you enjoy your trip across the Empire?" Lady Julianna interjected, leaning across her cousin. "We were so busy earlier on the tour, we never got to ask you."

Lady Lyriana was watching me again, her hazel eyes wide, a slight frown on her lips. Those pink, pouty lips….

I may not have been the most social Heir Apparent in the Empire, but I knew enough about the politics of friendship. If I stopped antagonizing Lord Tristan and made nice with Lady Julianna, it would warm Lady Lyriana up to me. But until my father's threat was off the table, I couldn't let that happen.

Knowing my father, I'd never be able to let that happen.

"Dull," I said. "Done it before. Didn't like it then, either."

"The trip across the Empire? Or the library?" Lady Lyriana asked.

The trip! Just the trip. I'd go to on a thousand tours of the library if you were leading them, I thought.

I gave a non-committal shrug and returned my attention to Tristan, not wanting to see Lyriana's face fall or grow angry. "Forgive me, my lord. We've been chatting so long, and I realized I never got your name. You were, after all, not one to come up and greet me upon my arrival."

"Lord Tristan Grey," he said, practically growling. "At your service."

"Hmmm," I said, already looking away. I raised my hand, snapping for a servant. One was by my side within seconds. "Mead?" I asked. "Or does Bamaria only serve wine?"

"We have plenty of bottles, your grace," she said nervously. "Do you prefer it iced or hot?"

"Hot please," I said. Then realizing I'd been polite with my *please,* I added, "Spice it." I dismissed her, slamming my elbows on the table and glaring at everyone around me.

Lady Lyriana watched me, offense in her eyes. I'd insulted her, her cousin, Lord Tristan, and now her serving staff.

I opened my mouth to vomit some sort of apology followed by a barrage of compliments because I could barely stand my own presence anymore, but then Imperator Kormac strolled to our end of the table.

"I wasn't able to properly say hello earlier," he drawled. "Your grace." He lowered his chin to Lady Meera in respect and gave small nods to Lady Morgana and Lady Lyriana. Without warning, he swiped his hand out, grabbing hold of Jules's wrist.

Lyriana stiffened beside me, and for the briefest moment, tension filled Jules's face before she broke out into a sunny smile. "Your highness," she said, sounding delighted. Jules was a consummate actress, but any noble could see the act for what it was. She was terrified of the southern Imperator.

"My lady." He tugged at her arm until she stood. "I was just sitting across the room with Imperator Hart and marveling at what a glorious dress you had on tonight. Might I have a look?" As he pulled her closer, Jules offered a quick, reassuring look at Lyriana, whose shoulders visibly fell. But underneath the table, she wrung her hands together nervously.

The Imperator's eyes trailed down the length of Jules's body before she was pushed away, his hand still grasping hers as he forced her to twirl in a circle. The drums paused, as the dancers came to the end of their first performance, and the dining hall erupted into applause.

"Well, now you've seen the dress," Jules said. "I thank you, your highness, for the compliment. I'm not worthy of such attention."

Not that Jules wasn't beautiful, but there was nothing special about her dress at all. Every woman in the room had on some variation of the same style. The low-cut gowns with high slits were staples in the south with its warm climate. The color of the dress, some kind of purple suited her skin tone—but again, it didn't stand out from any of the others.

A new beat started to play, slow and quiet. As more drummers steadily added their notes, the rhythm became more complicated until it was pounding.

Imperator Kormac sneered and gave a slight shake of his head. He wasn't going to let her go. What in fucking Lumeria! Dinner hadn't even been served. My father was a fucking animal, but he at least waited until dessert to pull this shit.

I glanced around the room at the adults, the nobles, the ones who were supposedly so righteous, so full of power and authority, so concerned with taking the moral high ground, and not a single one of them flinched or seemed surprised by the audacity of Imperator Kormac. They were all drinking, watching the dancers and musicians performing throughout the room.

I knew the rules. They had been drilled into me since birth.

An Imperator ruled over all. One word from an Imperator to the Emperor, one mistake reported, and he could end a life.

But to let him do this so openly to a noble, the niece of the Arkasva, who wasn't even past her Revelation Ceremony—was this not an insult to Arkasva Batavia himself? Yet he allowed it. Like he allowed Imperator Kormac's men to infiltrate his lands.

The more I saw, the more I realized Father could be right. Arkasva Batavia may very well be willing to allow his daughter to go north to secure his borders if his own niece was allowed to be so openly insulted without objection.

My stomach turned.

The servant I'd ordered to bring my mead returned. I grabbed it without offering thanks and brought it to my lips as I glanced around the room. Soturi lined the walls of the dining hall, all watching their various charges. Scowling in the corner, I recognized a bald soturion who'd followed Lady Lyriana's steps through the Library. Beside him was another soturion with a neatly trimmed beard, and short dark hair. His hands were tightened on the hilt of his sword and his jaw tense as his gaze remained on Lady Julianna. But even he didn't move, didn't dare to protect her, just as my personal escort had failed to protect me. There was no protecting against an Imperator.

But Avery Kormac wasn't my Imperator.

I took another sip of my mead. I was going to need to be drunk, or appear so, for what I planned.

The twisting in my stomach tightened. Would my father punish me for this? Yes. But if I did nothing, would he punish me? The chances were about the same.

Fuck it. Maybe I couldn't help my mother at home. But this…this I could do.

I slammed the drink on the table and ordered the servant to come back.

"Changed my mind. Ice it," I demanded. "Now."

The servant's bottom lip quivered, making me feel like the

biggest asshole in Lumeria, but she removed her stave from her belt pocket, and within seconds, my mead glass was frozen, the steam rising from the drink vanishing and leaving a cold breeze beneath my nose.

"Bring another," I ordered, lifting the drink to my lips and chugging. "Chilled."

If I was going to play this role, I was going all in.

Imperator Kormac had still not let go of Jules, and I could see Lyriana becoming more upset. She glanced around the room, her bottom lip pouting in a helpless way as she also began to register that no one was going to help her cousin. The ones in charge were drinking their wine and watching the performances, perfectly happy to be distracted.

I knew the powerlessness that came when those in authority did whatever the fuck they wanted, and in public, no less. No one stood up to them. No one dared to—out of fear, out of protocol, or out of the knowledge that the tides could turn against them.

But the tides had already turned against me. They'd been turned as long as I could remember. What did I have to lose?

A trickle of mead dripped down my chin as I finished my glass and slammed it on the table. Too loudly. Far from pious or proper or whatever else was supposed to describe an Heir to the Arkasva and Imperator.

If I was going to be beaten tonight, at least I'd pass out soon after.

The servant returned, a second chilled glass of mead in her hand. I grabbed it, wiped at my lips, and tilted my head back, chugging as quickly and sloppily as I could.

A wave of dizziness washed through me, and for a second, my head spun. I swore I saw stars glittering around Lyriana's head.

I swallowed the last of my drink, shoved the glass across the table to Lord Green. No, not green. Grey. Fuck. Lord Grey. I stood, stumbling toward the Imperator and Jules, who'd been cornered against the wall.

Lord Grey pushed my emptied glass away with disgust, wiped his fingers on a napkin, and stood, moving quickly to the other side of the table and into my empty chair. I hoped I'd left the seat warm.

He reached forward, taking Lyriana's hand in his, and at this, she visibly relaxed.

My chest tightened. He was doing nothing. Not helping Jules. Not doing a Godsdamned thing to stop the problem—to put an end to the reason why Lyriana was upset. But he got to comfort her. He got to play the fucking hero.

This was for the best. For all of us.

I stumbled forward, not even needing to act like I was drunk because, by the Gods, Bamarians had a heavy fucking hand in their mead. I fell back against the wall beside Jules, giving the Imperator from the south a conspiratorial look. He sized me up and down, and again, something inside me, some part of my soul, recognized him for what he was. A wolf in man's clothing. A monster.

"Thought you were going to come with me," I said. I leaned against Jules, my mouth far too close to her face to be proper. "I told you, you're my type." I winked, sliding my hand behind her back.

I offered Imperator Kormac a pleading look. Men like him, they were willing to release women they meant to harm, but only into the arms of another man who seemed intent on the same.

"I know you want to," I said to Jules, cringing as I spoke. It was something I'd heard other nobles say at parties, and I hated myself for saying it. Hated my whole fucking being. But I had to play the role. "You were flirting with me," I added, "in front of everyone."

Imperator Kormac rolled his eyes and released her hand,

stalking backward and then turning to rejoin my father, who was staring at me with a livid expression.

With the mead in my system, I'd probably pass out before he finished his beating. If it threw him off Lady Lyriana's scent as well, it would be worth it.

"I was being polite before, not flirting," Jules hissed. "But... thank you."

I almost blurted out, "I know," but I shook my head. "For what?" I asked. I had to keep playing my part. If I gave up now, the stunt would be useless.

"Should we...um...sit back down for the dinner?" Jules asked. She sounded scared, and my stomach twisted, knowing I could do nothing to ease her fears. Not right away, not if I was going to get her away from what she truly feared—the man who actually had an intent to hurt her. If I let her return, he'd bide his time, but he'd have her back in the corner by dessert, I was sure of it. And he'd never fall for my ruse again if I didn't follow through.

"I told you. You're coming with me." I tugged her arm.

Lady Lyriana sat next to Lord Grey looking worried. She reached for Lady Meera, who sat stoically, her back completely straight, her expression frozen into compliance.

I sneered at all the looks of derision and pity. But no one stopped me, nor did anyone object.

Just like home. Just like always. Those with more power didn't stand up for those with less, and so...this is what we resorted to.

I pulled Jules from the room into the hall.

"Get off of me," she seethed.

I'd already let her go. "I won't hurt you," I said, my voice low. "I won't touch you. But he was going to."

"I know," she said darkly. "He already has."

My jaw dropped, and I stepped back. Gods. Fucking bastard. "I'm sorry. Does Arkasva Batavia—?"

"No!" she yelled. "He doesn't. No one does. No one can do anything." She blinked rapidly, drawing back tears. "It's fine. I'm a big girl. I can handle myself. I may carry the name and blood of Ka Batavia in my veins, but without the protections afforded me by a diadem…I make the best of it."

"No one stops him?" My voice was shaking. "Ever?"

Her nostrils flared. "My escort tends to make an appearance at the last possible second. Before it goes," she squeezed her eyes shut, "too far."

He was too late even if he was stopping the worst from happening. I was too late. It wasn't enough. "You should be—" I cut myself off from saying *protected*. I felt a presence looming behind me, heard the quiet steps of leather boots.

I pressed my mouth to Jules's ear, trying not to be sick when she flinched from my touch. I needed to burn in hell, to have my soul eaten, to suffer whatever other horrible, fucked-up punishment existed. I deserved them all.

"We're being watched. Do you want to return to dinner? Be in the same room as him again?" I asked. Even if the Imperator wasn't done with her, even if it fucked up my attempt to draw attention away from Lady Lyriana, Julianna had every right to choose how she wanted to proceed.

Julianna tilted her head, her eyes wide with fear as she assessed me. "No. I don't."

"Do you trust me?" I asked.

She bit her lip, so similar to Lyriana's. "I probably shouldn't."

"You're probably right."

"You're kind of an asshole, you know."

"I know."

But she nodded. "Fine."

"Come to my room. You'll be safe there. I will not touch you. I swear." I stepped back and pressed my fist to my heart, tapping twice before laying my hand flat across my chest. "*Me sha, me ka.*" My oath, my soul.

Jules exhaled sharply at the suggestion of going to my room. "Fine."

"Good. Let's go." I released my hold on her, taking only her hand and moving quickly, praying I had each turn of the hall memorized. When I almost made a wrong turn, Jules was kind enough to correct me and point us in the right direction. But that delay allowed Bowen to catch up behind us.

At last, I reached my room. I slammed and locked the door behind me before releasing Jules.

"Now what?" she asked.

"Now nothing," I said, moving to the nightstand where a decanter full of water stood.

I poured myself a glass, needing to dull at least some of the effect the mead was having on me. Passing out would be great, but before that happened, I had to think at least somewhat straight. Somehow in my plan to convince my father I didn't have feelings for Lady Lyriana, I'd deprived Imperator Kormac —a man who ruled over a country known for seeing rape as a natural part of life—his prey. Rapists, I'd learned, weren't too far from akadim in their operation. If he didn't get what he wanted, he'd find it elsewhere, wherever, or whomever was easiest.

Everyone else down there was an heir or surrounded by immediate family. Everyone but Jules. Her parents had died; I remembered that now. She would have been—*had* been—the easiest pickings for the Imperator in a court of nobles.

"You can leave whenever you want," I said. "Or stay. All night if you want…if you need to. Bed's yours. I'll take the floor."

She wrapped her arms across her chest, looking cold despite the warmth of the night. "You're not what I expected."

"I find meeting expectations overrated."

"You're exactly what she thought, though. Or what she

hoped you were."

I froze. "What?"

"Lyr. She thinks underneath this cold exterior you present, you might actually be sweet for some reason. She said she saw something in you the last time you were here, and didn't believe it was gone."

My breath caught. The library. The cake. The boy who needed a friend.

"I told her she was farther than Lethea, especially with how you acted at the tour of the Great Library today, but..." Jules tapped her chin. "Now I think she might be right." She stepped forward, her gaze assessing as I tossed off my boots.

"She's not," I said, my voice full of scorn. "She was a child. She doesn't know the first fucking thing about me."

Jules stiffened. "Am I in danger from you?"

I exhaled. "No. But she's still wrong about me. Just because I'm not going to force myself on you—which is no compliment to me, by the way, only the bare minimum—doesn't mean I'm sweet or nice or worth anyone giving a shit over."

"Maybe." She shrugged. "But very few Heir Apparents I've come across have not taken advantage of their power and position at some point or another."

"Maybe I'm not like other Heir Apparents. Again, bare minimum. Is your cousin Lady Meera like other Heir Apparents?"

Jules shook her head. "No. Meera is also kind. But so is Lyr, almost to a fault. And she can see when that's true in another."

"That's ridiculous," I sneered, willing my heart to stop pounding, wanting to stop this, to ask Jules everything Lyriana had said about me, about my last visit. But I couldn't.

"You don't know her," Jules said defensively. "She's my best friend, not just my cousin. And I'm only telling you this because...because you helped me, and I don't believe this whole act you're doing. I think you like her. You've been ignoring her a little too hard for it to be natural. Trying too hard to appear disinterested. Plus, I've seen the way you look at her when you allow yourself. You haven't smiled once since you got here except when you walked into Cresthaven and first laid eyes on Lyr."

Auriel's fucking bane! Was there anyone out there who didn't know I wanted her?

"Why hide it?" she asked. "You'd be a powerful match for her. And despite how you acted at dinner, I don't think she'd object to you choosing to court her."

"I'm hiding nothing," I snapped, but even I knew how flimsy my words sounded. "And I'm not courting her. Not now. Not ever." Fuck. "Everyone thinks this?"

Jules shook her head. "No. You've been mostly rude and aloof, so that's what most people have seen. But I see it as my job to be extra vigilant with her. She's special."

I bit my lip. She was.

"And as she said, all nobles are liars."

"How do you know I'm not lying now?" I asked.

"You're trying to. But you're not. If you didn't care, you wouldn't have asked me."

I exhaled sharply. "You're a little too perceptive for your own good. You know that? You can call me Rhyan, by the way," I said. After all this, what was the point of using formalities?

"Jules. And thank you, I know," she said with a small smile. "Also, thank you for what you did downstairs. I'm in your debt. Is there anything I can do to repay the favor?"

I shook my head, but as I stared at the bed, my father's words came back to me.

And once Kane has put a baby in her belly, and her tits swell to twice their size....

Bowen was outside my door. He'd no doubt be reporting to my father what transpired here tonight.

"No," I said to Jules. "You don't need to repay me." I stared at the door. "Though, I hope you don't mind the consequences of this. I'm assuming...everyone at dinner will think we slept together by this point." Bowen would definitely tell my father Jules was alone in here with me. The door locked.

Jules bit her lip. "Maybe that's not such a bad thing. Maybe it will get the Imperator off my back for a little."

I watched her carefully. That was possible. And it could convince my father that my eye was elsewhere—keep him from looking at Lyriana as a way to manipulate me.

"But as soon as Lyr sees me," Jules said, "she'll know nothing happened."

"What if you lied to her," I said.

Jules laughed. "I can't do that. She knows me too well. This is stupid. Nothing happened. I don't care if people think it did. But I'm not going to pretend otherwise. And I'm not going to try to convince Lyr."

"You don't have to pretend it did—but," I said carefully, "what if you didn't go out of your way to let people know the truth."

"Why? So you can seem like a man?"

"If you think I give one shit about that, you don't know me at all. I don't give a damn what others think."

She narrowed her gaze. "That I actually believe. But, why? Rhyan, this is ridiculous."

"Maybe it's not," I said.

"Look, I don't really care what people think of me either. I'm not expected to keep up a perfect reputation like my cousins are. But I'm also not going to go around convincing everyone I'm another notch in your belt."

But if my father thought that's what happened, it might convince him I didn't care, or at least wouldn't be so easily manipulated.

"Jules," I pleaded. "This isn't for my reputation. Or my ego, or anything so frivolous. What if I told you that allowing everyone to believe we were together was to protect Lyriana?"

"Protect Lyriana? From what?" she asked, her voice serious.

"From me."

Jules shook her head. "You wouldn't hurt her."

I closed my eyes slowly. "I wouldn't. Would never. But there are others close to me…I can't say more than that. Just…I'm not a good person to be around. To get close to. People in my life… they get hurt. And it's always my fault."

Jules stared at me a long moment, her arms wrapped around her chest as she thought through my words.

"Imperators," Jules said at last, her voice hushed.

"Imperators," I said with a nod.

She bit her lip, seemingly grappling with her choice. "Is Lyr in danger?"

"If we go on with this charade…hopefully not."

"Fine."

I could take care of the rest. Despite what she'd seen in me those years before, Lady Lyriana was already looking at me in horror. If things continued the way they'd appeared to be going at dinner, Lord Grey would be falling to his knees and asking for her hand in marriage in a matter of months. I'd be back home in Glemaria, and I'd forget the clever hints of green and gold in her eyes, the way she smiled, the way her presence lit up the room, the way she—I'd forget her. I had to.

"I'm tired," I said.

"You can lie down," Jules said quietly. "In your bed. I'm not going to stay. Lyr will…she'll be looking for me. But I'll stay long enough for the other thing to be *believable,* for anyone else that might care."

"That would repay the debt," I said quickly. "Letting everyone believe. Please. Don't admit the truth if you can help it, and if you can't lie to Lady Lyriana about this, just, speak to her in private."

She rolled her eyes. "I grew up in a court of liars. I know how to keep a secret, Lord Rhyan. I'll keep yours. That you're actually a decent fucking human being."

"If that's what you believe. As long as Lyriana thinks I'm an ass, we're good."

I watched her make her way onto my balcony, gripping the bars and staring at the night sky. Her shoulders shook. She was crying. Fuck. I moved to comfort her, but just as quickly as the shaking began, it stopped. I debated going out to her, but the moment seemed private. So I stayed back.

I laid across the blankets on my bed, my eyes closing easily from exhaustion over the past few weeks and the extremely potent mead I'd inhaled without any food.

When I opened my eyes, it was pitch black inside my room. The only light came from the fading torches hissing on the outer turrets of Cresthaven.

"Jules?" I asked into the dark. "Lady Julianna?" There was no answer. She'd left like she'd said she would.

I stumbled into the adjoining bathroom to piss. As I stumbled back to bed, I replayed the events of the night in my mind, pausing on the absolute farther than Lethea moment I'd decided to take away what an Imperator wanted, to come between him and his prey.

I didn't regret it. Not for a second. Jules deserved to be saved, deserved so much more than anyone was giving her. One day soon, her escort wouldn't arrive at the last possible moment; he'd be too late, and the Imperator would drag her away. Or worse, the Bastardmaker.

By the Gods, let my actions have protected Lyriana, not made things worse.

Her eyes flashed in my mind again—alluring, clever, mischievous, seductive. For a second, the hazel color transformed, her irises turning gold. I saw her clearly—her skin darkening, her hair as red as flames—and then her face righted itself, looking just as it had when I'd first seen her in the Seating Room up close.

My eyes closed, and I was lost to a dreamless sleep.

CHAPTER
FIVE

I awoke to the sounds of my door creaking open and leather boots stomping on the floor, a raging headache pounding in my skull, and some part of my soul twisting, already knowing what was about to happen.

"Rough night?" my father asked.

Sunlight burned red against my closed eyes. The room grew brighter as he opened every closed curtain in the room.

Now he opened them. Now he let in the light and breeze.

I pressed my palm to my forehead, slightly nauseated as the night's events flashed through my mind. The way everyone in the dining hall with power had allowed Jules to be attacked by Kormac without a word of protest or intervention. The way Lady Lyriana had looked so hopeless, helpless.

"The hell you think you're playing at?" my father asked. Cold filled the room, swirling like a hurricane around me. His aura wasn't just pulsing, it was vibrating, tense and ready to attack.

I opened my eyes slowly, sat up, and braced myself, my fingers curling into the sheets of my bed. "Good morning to you, your highness."

"So now we're in the business of undermining Imperators?"

"I have never undermined you, your highness. I am a loyal son to Glemaria. And to you. Father."

"You Godsdamned childish fool. You know damn well what I meant. What's gotten into you?"

I bit the inside of my cheek, my body stiff with tension, trying to summon any ounce of bravery I had, any part of me that remembered what it was to be a cocky, spoiled noble. "I wanted her. So I took her. Isn't that the way?" My vision went in and out of focus from the pain in my head.

"You fuck her?"

I glared. "She's not an heir to the Seat of the Arkasva. She's less than a spare. As you well saw."

"Did you fuck her?" he asked again, emphasizing each word.

"Yes."

He laughed. "She has a birthmark shaped like an almond. Just below her left breast. Did you see? Did you touch it? Did it you taste it?"

My fingers curled. "How would you know? Did you touch her?"

He made a face of disgust. "After you? Of course, not. I found something fresh."

"Then—" I froze. Imperator Kormac. I felt sick.

My father stalked toward my bed, grabbed my blankets, and pulled them off in one sweeping motion, letting them fall to the floor. I was nearly naked, shivering in only my underwear, as the temperature in the room dropped violently.

"Lady Julianna has that birthmark on top of her left breast," he said. "Where anyone can see with these whore-dresses they wear. Surely you didn't miss that."

My chest tightened, every part of my body filling with goosebumps, my limbs beginning to shake. "It was dark, your highness. The fuck do you care?"

"I care because I think you're playing games. I think you've gotten bold now that we're in another country. And I think it's time you're reminded of your place."

I squeezed my eyes shut, barely noticing his grip on my wrists, the sound I made when my back hit the floor, the feel of his boots on my ribs, the metallic taste of blood on my tongue, or the way yesterday's drink and food filled my mouth before it spilled onto the floor.

My chest heaved. Pain pounded inside me, sliced through me. My eyes burned as my father cursed beneath his breath.

And then it was over.

"Clean yourself up, son." His voice was gentle. Soothing. "Come downstairs and eat breakfast with your father. You'll feel better when you have some real food in your belly, I promise. Let's see you put some weight on, all right. How are you going to be a soturion in the fall if you don't get any meat on those bones?" He paused. "And, Rhyan," he added, speaking my name with affection, "the next time you want to fuck a girl, try getting your dick hard."

The door slammed behind me, and I lay on my side on the floor, holding my knees to my chest, shaking.

Half an hour later, I was the epitome of the miserable, callous, asshole Heir Apparent to the Arkasva and Imperator at breakfast. I found my inner cocky, uncaring noble self, and I burrowed into my role. I didn't speak to a single soul or look at anyone present. Not my father, not Imperator Kormac, not even Jules to check on her, especially not Lady Lyriana.

The one glimmer of light in this whole disaster had been my father's failure to mention her this morning. Not that his silence on the subject meant he hadn't connected the dots between my actions last night and protecting her, but I needed some indication that good had come of what I'd done. That at least this morning's beating, if not all the others, had accomplished something. That in the end, there was a reason for all of this.

I chewed my food without tasting it, grimacing as every

swallow and small movement made my ribs hurt. At least this breakfast did not involve the full Bamarian Council and Lord Grey watching me with all of his disdain and snobbery as he made his obviously calculated advances toward Lady Lyriana.

The moment it was over, I returned to my room, walked out onto my balcony, and stared at the ocean, watching the waves crash against the shore and fall back, again and again. The Bamarian clocktowers rang out their hour, and moonstone-blue lights flashed across the sky, the magic creating the steps for the ashvan horses to race across.

Most Lumerians thought ashvan could fly. They mistook the sky creatures for acting like seraphim or gryphons, creatures with wings. But ashvan had no wings. They had magic in their hooves. Magic that laid down steps again and again and again. Wherever the ashvan needed to go, the magic supported them, was always there for them, creating every single step, providing sure footing.

What I wouldn't give for something like that. A supported path. A road. A way to escape. A guarantee that my next step would be safe, that I wasn't heading into disaster, about to fall.

As the blue lights and jewel-toned manes of the ashvan disappeared, leaving behind a clear blue sky with the kind of fluffy, brilliant pastel clouds you only saw in the summer, I continued to stare at the waves, to try to calm myself and distract myself from feeling pain.

When the hour came again, I was startled out of my trance.

There was a knock on my door. My hands gripped the balcony railing, my knuckles white.

"Your grace," called Bowen. The door creaked open, and his footsteps echoed behind me. "It smells delightful in here," he said casually.

I'd cleaned up my vomit after my father had left—not trusting a maid to be silent—but the smell still lingered. A reminder. I had to be more careful. I had to keep my temper in check.

"You don't find the scent of vomit invigorating?" I asked.

"Invigorating. Perhaps a different word choice?"

I turned around. "What do you want, Bowen?"

"You have a visitor."

For a moment, my heart leapt at the thought that it was Lady Lyriana. But I quickly slammed that down. Why in Lumeria would she come to see me? I'd been nothing but a gryphon-shit asshole to her since I'd arrived, and hopefully, she was convinced I'd been an even bigger asshole to her favorite person in the world last night. Maybe that was who—Jules? To check-in and let me know what was happening with our agreement, if we even still had one? She hadn't exactly promised anything, but I was pretty sure we were on the same page—keep Lyriana safe.

"Rhyan," a warm voice with a thick Glemarian accent burst into my room.

A weight lifted from me as I recognized the voice's owner.

I rushed off the balcony and straight into the arms of Uncle Sean. Technically, he was my cousin once removed on my father's side, but he'd always been an uncle to me. Born in Glemaria and proud, but also kind and caring, Sean was the opposite of my father in every way.

He hugged me tight to him, his aura like a Glemarian forest —soft, still, familiar. I hadn't seen him in a year. He'd left our country to move here, wanting to be as far from my father as possible. They'd never gotten along.

I winced even as I sank into him.

"Oh, my boy," he said, shaking his head. "This heat does not agree with you." He pushed my hair off my forehead, his face grim.

It wasn't the heat, but he knew that. And we both knew that moving across the Empire wasn't going to save him from my father's wrath if he dared say more.

"Does the Imperator know you're here?" I asked.

"Of course. Your father knows all," he said, eyes crinkling. They were green, like the eyes of most of Ka Hart. A subtle forest green, a normal green—not like mine. "Come. Let's get out of here. Have you been down to the beach?"

"We do have those at home," I said dryly. I headed back to my balcony, Sean on my heels.

Laughter rang out below. As I gazed down at the shore, I saw Jules looking happy, unaffected from the night before and—my heart swelled—Lyr. Lyriana. Lady Lyriana. Her hair was fiery with flames beneath the sun. Lady Meera and Lady Morgana were with them, all four shedding their robes to reveal brightly colored bathing suits as they raced into the waves of the ocean. Like every time I saw her, I swore the lights dimmed. This time, it was the sun itself. My focus succumbed to flames on the clear blue tides of the water. Lady Lyriana's hair blew wildly in the breeze as she waded deeper, catching a small wave. Fire and water mixed.

"This one seems to have a little more excitement. Plus, your beaches are all rocks," said Sean. "And cold."

"*Our* beaches," I said pointedly.

"Right." He glanced away. "Rhyan, you know I'm not coming back."

I bit the inside of my cheek. Sean was one of the few members of my father's family I could stand. He was the only one who ever seemed to be on my side, who cared. And now he was as far from me as he could get. My gut twisted, but I forced myself to swallow, to keep my face trained to a neutral expression.

"Did she say yes?" I asked.

When last he'd written to me, Sean had fallen in love with a Bamarian mage, a lesser noblewoman of Ka Drona. I'd hoped he'd convince her to relocate to Glemaria, but he was clearly going to remain here, perhaps less from his lack of convincing and more from his desire to stay away.

"She did," he said.

My throat tightened. *"Tovayah maischa.* When's the wedding?"

Sean smiled. "Thank you. Fall."

"I'll be starting soturion training. He'll never…I'll miss it."

He nodded sadly. My father would also not be attending.

"All right, that's enough serious talk. We're in the south. It's summer. We have sun! Now, what do you say? Should we go for a swim? Take a walk?"

I turned back to the waters, my gaze immediately finding her, like I knew instinctively where to look, like I couldn't look at anyone or anywhere else.

Lady Lyriana emerged from the waves, water dripping down her body of golden curves glowing beneath the sun. A wave rose, rolling toward the shore, cresting and falling just behind her, making it look as if she wore a gown of shimmering blue water.

A small crowd of mages approached the shoreline, Lord Grey among them. I recognized the pretentious walk at once, the brown floppy hair shined to perfection. Too many escorts. Who the fuck did he think he was?

"This beach is too crowded," I said, turning abruptly to go inside.

Sean chuckled. "Still not a people person."

I glared.

"Don't worry. I had another one in mind to show you," he said, jerking his chin toward my door. His hand landed on my back, and as I grimaced in pain, he immediately pulled back, his familiar eyes searching mine before they shifted, his nose crinkling as he sniffed the room.

"Your alternative beach it is," I said quickly.

Sean gave a small smile. "Grab your sandals, and let's go. Ah, Soturion Bowen, fancy a seraphim flight?"

Half an hour later, the floor of our seraphim carriage shifted, cool wind blowing into our windows pushing my hair into my eyes. With a thud, we touched the ground, our giant, golden-winged bird laying down on her belly as the blue carriage doors opened and a small set of stairs descended onto the golden sand of Gryphon Island. Giant waves crashed against the shore, wild as if powered by the magic said to still reside in the sunken continent of Lumeria Matavia deep beneath the ocean.

"It's got sand. And water," I said dryly, stepping around some dried seraphim shit. "I'll give you that."

"It also has this," Sean said, pointing ahead.

Bowen grumbled behind me as his leather boots slipped on a mound.

I held my hand over my eyes to block the sun's glare, and then I saw it. The Guardian of Bamaria, a statue of a gryphon carved out of three stories' worth of black onyx, sat on the shore with its paws before it, watching, waiting. For what, no one knew. The statue was famous, one of the most well-known works of art in Lumeria and one of its greatest mysteries.

"Do you like it?" Sean asked.

"I've seen bigger."

He snorted. "You always loved gryphons. Figured you should see the most famous statue of one."

I bit the inside of my cheek, not wanting to admit he was right. In truth, I'd read all about the Guardian of Bamaria. One of my scrolls I'd brought along for the trip had been a history of the statue and all known theories surrounding it. Historians had been theorizing for years on why such a massive structure symbolic of the Kavim and animals who preferred the north had been built in the south. It would have been more fitting for the Guardian to have been a seraphim given Ka Batavia's love for the creatures.

Another oddity, or perhaps a coincidence I couldn't explain, was that in Glemaria, we had a seraphim statue on Gryphon's Mount built of pure moonstone. It was a structure that should have been created for Bamaria. One theory had been that the twin statues were end caps of the Empire, symbolizing the southernmost and northernmost ports. But neither statue was in the correct location geographically for this to be true. The other popular theory was that it was a symbol of friendship between the Kavim. There were a ton of conspiracy theories about secrets inside the statues, none of which felt plausible to me.

Sean was right. I *was* interested in seeing the statue. It had actually been on a list of things I wanted to see in the Empire I'd once written as a boy. I'd missed it last time, not being able to leave the fortress, my father refusing to take me anywhere.

I should have asked Lady Lyriana about this on the tour. I'd have bet anything she knew exactly where every scroll written about the Guardian was located.

I moved quickly over the sand dunes sprinkled across our path. Bowen stayed back, taking his stance beside our resting seraphim, allowing Sean and I some privacy for once. I supposed on an empty beach, the threat to my life was small. And if my father decided to show up, Bowen was perfectly happy to stand back and let him do his worst.

The Guardian loomed above me, casting a shadow across the sand. I stepped forward and slid my hand across an onyx haunch.

The wind blew with such sudden force and speed, I almost stumbled back.

"Looks like a storm's coming," Sean said.

"There was no indication before."

He frowned, and I stepped back to stare up at the gryphon's massive head. The waves behind me calmed.

"They sure don't come in this size back home," he said.

I shrugged.

"Can you imagine a rope holding this one down?" he asked.

"If it's like any other gryphon, yes," I replied.

"If it was a smart gryphon, it would look in the mirror and see how huge it is and definitely not let a rope keep it."

I shrugged again, as another gust of wind blew against us, sand running over my boots.

"Are you all right?" Sean asked.

"Over some wind?"

"Rhyan," he said, voice serious. "Are you...are you all right?"

I knew what he meant, but I couldn't bear to voice the truth out loud. Saying it made it real. Made it hurt. But if he said it, if he asked what he needed to ask....

But he wouldn't. He never did. No one ever fucking did.

"I have cured sunleaves in my bag," he said quietly. "Whatever happened this time, whatever he...I can help."

"And the next time I need fucking sunleaves?" I asked. "What then? You're on the other side of the Empire—you couldn't be farther away from me unless you went into Afeyan lands."

"I want to help you," he said, voice low.

Then ask. Ask! Fucking ask. Don't make me say it. Don't pretend it's fine. Don't hint at what we both know is true. Don't try to appease me with sunleaves. Say it. Ask it. Just fucking do it. Don't make me be the one.

I felt tears burning behind my eyes. Shame. A knot in my stomach. His hands on my back again. The complete loss of control over my expression, my mask falling, my desperation out in the open for Sean to see.

"I can't...." Sean trailed off, his Glemarian accent so heavy, I was almost ashamed after weeks of attempting to conceal mine. "I—" He swallowed. "Rhyan, I'm fighting to speak. But I'm bound. I...." He gritted his teeth. "Rhyan, I can't."

I understood. A blood oath. A Moriel fucking blood oath. Sean knew what my father was doing to me, and he couldn't speak a word about it. If he did, if he broke the oath, the magic imbued in the promise would destroy him.

"Sean, fuck. Why'd you bring me here?" I asked.

"I wanted to see you. See if you were all right. See you…see you away from him. From his guard."

"And say nothing?" I asked, my stomach twisting.

"I'm saying everything I can say!" he yelled. "I brought you here because, because I remember the boy you were. The one who loved gryphons more than anything. The boy who wanted a pet gryphon, who followed around the Master of the Horse to learn to care for them. The boy who was so full of love and hope despite having such a cold, cruel sire. I wanted to help you remember the boy who loved history and loved to read. The boy who would have raced to this statue the moment he learned about it. The boy who—the boy who I still love with my whole heart. I'm still your uncle, even over here." Tears brimmed in the corner of his eyes. "Distance doesn't change that. Rhyan, you're still my nephew."

"I'm not that boy anymore." He'd died a long time ago.

Uncle Sean blinked slowly, frowning, his shoulders falling in defeat.

"No," he said at last. "You're not. But that doesn't mean he isn't still somewhere deep down inside of you, hurting. That doesn't mean…." He shook his head. "I see the way you carry yourself now, the faces you make, like a replica of him."

"I am not my father!"

Uncle Sean grabbed my shoulders, his grip tight but not painful. He wouldn't hurt me. But I was sick of being restrained, sick of being told how to feel—told not to feel. Sick of everyone older, bigger, and stronger thinking they had power over me.

My back pressed against the warm onyx of the Guardian, anger bursting through me, as a burning-hot fury rushed through my veins. The sensation sliced through my entire body. With a yell, I shoved Sean back, feeling even more heat rise inside me.

His hold on me was gone in an instant. But he didn't just stumble away from me, he went flying backwards, his body soaring several feet in the air before his body smacked into a sand dune.

"Sean!" I yelled, racing forward, my body going cold. "I'm sorry. I didn't mean—"

He jumped to his feet, brushing sand from his soturion cloak. "Auriel's bane, Rhyan."

"Are you—I—" I stared at my hands. They looked normal. I felt normal. The anger inside of me was gone. Where in Lumeria had that strength come from?

"You pushed me." He sounded astonished. Not mad but as if he were impressed.

"I'm sorry," I said, opening and closing my hands. I'd never pushed anyone before. I'd never hit anyone. I'd never fought back.

"Rhyan," Sean said slowly, walking forward. "You just sent an anointed soturion flying." His gaze narrowed. "Not that I'm the greatest warrior in the Empire, but," he shook his head, stretching his arm back to rub the nape of his neck, "that shouldn't have been possible. Did your father—did he have your Birth Bind removed early?"

My mouth fell open. That would have explained the sudden surge of strength, but I'd been rebound almost instantly. The power was under my skin, unable to express itself, free itself, or be used. I could sense it, feel it stirring, feel it itching. But it was trapped. I'd never done anything or felt anything like this before.

I nodded, still in shock. "He put the Birth Bind on right after it was removed. I can't touch it, can't use it. The power I had, it's not mine. Not yet."

I turned back to the Guardian of Bamaria, my heart pounding faster. I touched the onyx, braced myself for it to happen again— the feeling of burning power breaking free, the sudden influx of wind and tide and storm that seemed to be brewing inside me and out.

Nothing happened.

"Maybe it was just a moment of anger," I said. "That can happen right? A sudden surge? Energy accumulating?"

Uncle Sean eyed the gryphon and me suspiciously. "I don't know. Has anything like this ever happened before? Have you ever hit him?"

I shook my head, embarrassed.

"It's okay, Rhyan. You didn't do anything wrong here, all right?"

I nodded, still unsure.

Sean stiffened suddenly, his eyes moving beyond the statue, and the sound of someone whistling began to swell in volume, rising over the rolling waves and wind of the ocean.

I stilled, seeing an Afeyan woman walking slowly over the water. I'd gone most of my life barely ever seeing them, and this was my second sighting of an immortal in two days.

What was she doing here? Afeya had the most powerful magic in Lumeria—they were not bound to the waters as a source of power like we were. They weren't even bound by our laws. All Afeya possessed the power of all the vorakh—seeing the future, mind-reading, and, mine, traveling. The Afeya I'd seen at the library had to have traveled. One second, he'd been right there, and the next, he'd vanished.

I couldn't help but feel like prey, like this Afeya was prowling for a victim, looking to strike a deal.

"We should probably head back," Sean said, his hand slowly moving to grip the hilt of his sword.

The Afeya's melodic whistle grew louder, and I looked over. She had long silky hair that was deep red, almost purple in color. She turned toward me, her body barely concealed by her dress. It seemed to be made entirely of small shells strung together. Each string originated from her shoulders and fell down her body. She was completely covered and somehow naked all at once, a flash of skin revealed and concealed with every step she took. A soft wind blew, the shells hanging across her body tinkling with movement that left me shivering.

Her eyes, violet, flashed on me and Sean, a coy smile on her lips, before she frowned and looked behind her. Another Afeya approached.

This one was male with long black hair, his body uncovered save for a golden loincloth, his skin blue and sparkling. A turn of his head and I stilled with recognition. I'd seen him at the library watching Lady Lyriana. Watching me.

He pointed a finger at the female Afeya and shook his head as if she were a child who'd disobeyed his orders. His eyes then focused on me again, and a feeling of fear, of dread, washed over my body. He grinned with that same feline smile from yesterday, like a pleased cat who'd laid out his mouse trap. He turned, and the female Afeya began to follow him, no longer on the water, but on the sand.

As she walked, her shells chimed. The sand beneath her feet remained untouched by her steps, leaving behind not one single footprint.

Not yet, my young lord.

The voice. The same voice from yesterday, melodic, haunting. It was in my head again. My whole body shivered with cold.

Sean remained still as the scene unfolded. As the two Afeya continued to move away from us, he relaxed his grip on his sword, his hand flexing at his side.

"Do they come into Bamaria often?" I asked.

"Not in the parts I frequent." Sean exhaled sharply. "We should get back. Your father only agreed for you to go on a short outing. So let me get this out before," he jerked his head back at Bowen, "before we have even more company."

I scanned the horizon, wary of more Afeya and members of my father's guard. "What?"

"I know the trappings placed upon you, the life you've been

afforded as the Heir to the Arkasva and Imperator. I'm not blind. I know your hands are tied, just as mine are."

"No, you don't," I said, barely able to hide the bitterness in my voice. "You escaped. You're here. You're free. I'll never leave Glemaria."

"You don't know what you'll do. Your future is not written in stone, Rhyan. It is not still, nor is it stagnant. It's not this statue behind you. Do you hear me? Your fate has not been determined. I know you didn't ask to be born into this family, to have him as a father. But you still get to choose how your life plays out."

"No, I don't. I can't," I said, my voice hoarse. "And even if I could…I can't leave her there alone. By herself."

"I know. I know you can't. Not right now. But I swear to you, if I could do more, I would, so I'm doing what I can. ME sha, me KA." He pressed his fist to his heart, tapped it twice, and flattened his palm—the sacred oath of Glemaria. "I may be in Bamaria, but my heart will always be of the north. If you ever find yourself in a position where you have to or want to leave, promise me you'll come to Bamaria. Help will always be offered to you. No questions asked. Anything you ever need. I swear."

"I'll probably end up like him one day. A miserable fucking asshole sitting on a cold golden Seat."

"You won't." He leaned in. "I remember your father as a boy. Devon was…Devon was always who he was going to be. You're not him. If you can do one thing for me—think of it as an early wedding present—then do this." He gripped my shoulder once more, softer than before. "Now, don't throw me this time."

"That's the present?" I eyed his hands on me.

He chuckled. "No. This is—remember who you are, Rhyan. Yes, your blood is his blood, but it's also mine. You are not him, and you never will be. Don't let him dictate who you are going to become. He dictates enough already."

I laughed, the sound mirthless and hopeless. "How?"

"With your mind. You have control of your mind. Your

thoughts. Maybe you can't control what he thinks, but you can control what you do. I know you have no say in what he does, but you can decide how you react. Whatever he says, whatever he does, it does not define you. Only you do that."

It sounded nice, but it didn't make any sense. "How?" I asked again.

Sean shrugged. "You threw me off you."

"And? That was a fluke."

Sean tilted his head. "Maybe it was, maybe it wasn't. But you don't know yet what you're capable of doing. Neither does he. Today proved it. Just keep yourself open to possibilities. That's the important thing. Stay open to the fact that you do not yet possess all the strength you will have. You will grow stronger, and you need to remember that very soon, your Birth Bind will be permanently removed, and no matter what it feels like now, your father is no God. He has chinks in his armor. He will not stay in power forever. I promise. Just give it time."

Bowen trekked toward us, kicking clouds of sand as he moved. In the distance, bells rang—another hour had passed— and blue lights soared across the sky.

I stared at the ashvan, at the steps appearing right where they were needed, keeping them from falling. Again and again. The magic perfect, supportive.

Would mine be the same? Would it help me when it was finally unleashed? Or just curse me all over again?

"You've tied his grace up with your silly ramblings enough, Sean," Bowen sneered as he approached us.

"This is why I'm more welcome in the south," Sean said quietly. "My mouth is too big." He clapped me on the shoulder. "Give your uncle at least this." His lips quirked into a half-smile. "The Guardian of Bamaria, it was worth the trip."

I bit the inside of my cheek, the backs of my eyes burning, the ashvan beginning to descend as another tide rose. "It was worth the trip."

CHAPTER
SIX

The following weeks passed by as slowly and torturously as had the litter ride across the Empire. I couldn't decide which was worse, being trapped inside those four tiny walls for endless hours with my father or the daily attendance at Arkasva Batavia's Court listening to petitions and enduring the moments Lady Lyriana arrived in formal attendance.

I tried not to look at her, but there were times I felt her eyes on me—a sensation I could not explain—and I'd find myself unable to stop my gaze from drifting toward her. Our eyes meeting across the room. Then I'd be wracked with guilt and fear. Everything good was always ruined for me; everything I ever cared about had a way of turning against me or being twisted by my father. Everything I ever touched turned to shit when he was around. The people I loved were hurt because of me. It was always my fault in the end.

The longer I spent in Arkasva Batavia's Court, the Ka Hart gryphon emblazoned in silver thread across the chest of my pressed black tunic, the more I knew I needed to forget Lady Lyriana. Banish her from my mind. My heart. My soul.

There was no point in caring about or for anyone or anything else. Not until he was gone. Not until I was free. If I ever would be.

My only small glimmers of hope came from the fact that Imperator Kormac had only stayed a week, and I'd heard not one more word about the engagement of Lady Lyriana to Arkturion Kane or any other gryphon-shit asshole in the north.

I'd taken to stalking the halls when not dining or standing in Court. I'd keep an ear open when I neared any group of gossiping nobles or crowd of servants. Servants always knew the stories before anyone else. If any betrothals had been arranged, someone in the fortress would know about it and gossip. And if Lady Lyriana knew, surely there'd be some shift in her demeanor or conversations.

Her noble mask had slipped enough times that if she were engaged and unhappy about it, I'd see some clue. Or if she were engaged and happy about it, I was sure that would show, too. Yet, daily, my findings turned up empty.

Plus, every few days or so, I'd check in with Jules. Ask her if there was anything new to report. She always said the same thing. There wasn't. And though Lyriana was well aware that nothing had happened between us, Jules also said that she didn't seem as convinced as before that I was a good person.

But over the last few weeks, I had more moments where I slipped, where I was weak. Where my gaze fell on her, drank her in, memorized her every slope and curve and the subtle shift of color in her hair or the darkening of her skin as summer progressed and she spent more time at the beach, laughing with her sisters and cousins and Lord fucking Tristan as they raced into the waves.

What I wouldn't have given to be out there with them. With her. To let it all go. To be free. To have fun. To…to feel.

I stayed on the balcony of my room, watching her disappear

into the glimmering waters, listening to the waves and their laughs crashing against the shores.

When I did catch myself slipping and watching her, I cursed myself and pulled my gaze away. I turned my attention back to the petitioners lined up to speak to Arkasva Batavia or to my dinner if we were dining or to my endless glasses of mead.

There was only one significant encounter between us during those weeks. I was walking down the hall after midnight, knowing Bowen was my shadow. The sun had been brutal all day, and even as night fell, the temperatures remained hot. Though my room had a cooling system and a breeze was carrying itself through my open windows, I hadn't been able to shake the sensation of heat from my body. I had been itching all over, restless, replaying the moment I pushed Uncle Sean and what it had meant. I'd thought it was the heat disturbing me, but I was beginning to suspect my power was starting to bubble over, straining against the replacement Birth Bind. I was going to go mad soon.

I'd tried cooling off on my balcony, or letting a scroll lull me to sleep. Then I threw myself on the floor completing a set of one hundred push-ups. And then another set. Nothing worked.

So, I started pacing the halls and found myself thinking of Lady Lyriana and walking down the stairs into the Great Hall of Cresthaven. Alongside me, the painted columns depicted pictures of the ancient bloodline of Ka Batavia that went back a thousand years. The hall was a splash of color. It felt heavy, ancient. Powerful.

It was also not empty.

Lady Lyriana stood in the center of the hall, staring up at a column, her hair dark beneath the moon and torchlights crackling and hissing from the walls. She'd pulled the long strands into a braid down her back, but there were loosened waves and curls falling out as if she'd been tossing and turning in her bed, too.

She wore a simple white night dress and had wrapped a red blanket around her shoulders. It was a bright, deep shade of red I knew they referred to as Batavia red, the same shade Lady Lyriana's hair turned in the sun.

I slowed before taking the final step into the hall, sensing Bowen pausing several feet behind me. Fucking traitor. I watched Lady Lyriana stare up at the column in adoration, her shoulders slowly rising and falling as if she were taking deep breaths. I knew two guards were stationed outside the double doors leading into the fortress. And I suspected there were around a half dozen stationed down the hall with their eyes trained on her.

My heart lurched as she turned, her clever eyes immediately finding mine, full of recognition though I stood away from her in the shadows.

"Lord Rhyan," she said politely, formally. As she always did. She lifted her chin in defiance, her eyes only briefly flicking to her state of informal dress before they met mine again. She offered a quick curtsey, looking me up and down. "Your grace."

I stepped off the stairs, landing in the same spot she jumped to the day we'd arrived. "Your grace," I said in return. I still worried about saying her name, worried I'd like saying it too much, worried I'd say it with too much emotion.

"I was not expecting to see anyone at this hour."

"I would say the same," I said, taking a tentative step forward.

She bit her lip, her beautiful, pouty lip, devoid of the lip color she wore to Court but still a tantalizingly delicious shade of pink. "Is there anything I can do for you?" she asked.

I raised my eyebrows. "Do for me? You're an Heir to the Arkasva. Were you going to fan me all night? Or plump my pillow?"

"Is that what you're looking for?"

I shrugged. "Depends who's offering."

She sucked in a breath. "I can't say that I'm particularly skilled in night fanning, or pillow plumping. However, as I am Heir to the Arkasva, and you are in my fortress, I am your host. And you are my guest; therefore, if you had need of such services, I could certainly order them for you."

A small shift of movement caught my eye in the shadows of the hallway leading to the Seating Room. A guard. Perhaps her miserable, personal escort, the scowling bald man.

I needed to leave her at once. Any of her guards could be bought by my father or Imperator Kormac. Bowen had been bought already. In case my father was still considering a marriage contract, I had to continue playing my role. Either way, I'd played for this long.

But I couldn't walk away.

"Simply a restless night, your grace. It's too damn hot in your country," I said.

"As much as I wish to keep the guests of Cresthaven comfortable, I am unfortunately not in control of the weather. I apologize that the south is not, in fact, the north. Or perhaps you'd be cool."

"Did it ever occur to you that maybe you're simply not trying hard enough to control the weather?" I asked, conspiratorially.

Her lips quirked. She almost smiled. I had to suppress mine.

"Perhaps another request?" she asked. "I can't cool the country for you, but perhaps I can cool you with a cold glass of water? Would that suffice in helping you to attain the comfort you require to sleep, your grace?"

My throat was dry. And I *was* too damn hot.

"Water sounds fantastic." I bowed. "I'll find my way to the kitchen."

Lady Lyriana rolled her eyes. "No, you won't. Follow me."

I bit the inside of my cheek, but I followed. This was innocent. This was just going for a glass of water. She marched toward the kitchens and straight into the cold room where they had water on tap. I expected her to call for one of the staff to serve us, but she seemed to know her way around as she gathered two glasses and filled them both.

"Here you are, Lord Rhyan," she said as she handed me my glass.

I reached out, my fingers brushing against hers, some kind of tingling rising in my skin. I was touching her. The most I'd ever touched her. Fingers against fingers. Her skin on mine. It sent my heart racing, my blood pumping. It wasn't enough. I wanted more. I wanted to hold her hand. I wanted to touch her arm, her hair, her…everywhere. And yet, if this was all I ever got, it was everything.

She watched our hands, her mouth falling open.

The glass almost slipped, but I grasped it, releasing my fingers from hers, still feeling the buzzing feeling inside, still feeling her touch. I took a sip as she did the same, her eyes wide and watching me like I was the biggest piece of gryphon-shit in Lumeria.

Fuck. I had to get it together.

We both swallowed, lowering our glasses together. Her mouth started to open, and then she raised her glass again, taking a long sip. I did the same.

When we lowered our glasses a second time, she started to look away.

"Thank you," I said formally. Without another word, I left the room with my water, my hand shaking as I made my way back to my bedroom. I stood out on the balcony, drinking the glass she had poured for me though I had a perfectly chilled decanter of water beside my bed. I closed my eyes, listening to the waves crashing against the shores, my skin beginning to cool and the itch beneath my skin beginning to fade.

It had been nothing. A moment. We'd both been cold and formal to each other except for that one slip. But as I took my final swallow of water and retreated to my bed, my fingers still tingling from hers, a new heat rose inside me. Not the heat of summer, but the fire of her touch.

I flexed my hand and made a fist, still feeling the sensation of her skin against mine. I couldn't get back to sleep then if I tried. I slid out of my night-shorts, and gripped myself between my legs, knowing I was touching myself with the same hand that had touched hers. At least I was enjoying the restlessness for once.

A few days passed without event. Lady Lyriana made no indication we had seen each other or talked. As with that moment all those years ago in the library, I expected her finding a restless lord in need of water after midnight meant nothing.

But the day before Bamaria's solstice celebration, as the final petitioner was heard and Arkasva Hart completed the day of Court, I rounded the corner and found Jules waiting for me. She'd been eyeing me all session, and I was worried it meant something had happened.

Or that Lady Lyriana had mentioned running into me.

"Your grace," Jules said politely. Her long brown hair had been pulled back into an intricate braid. It was not a detail I tended to notice, but Lady Lyriana had been wearing hers in the same style—full of little golden beads, neat, and shiny. A far cry from the messiness of her hair the other night.

"Back to your grace? And here I thought we'd moved beyond the formal terms of address." I smirked and bowed. "Well, then, how doth my lady?"

"Cut the crap, Rhyan," Jules snapped. "After all, I'm not your lady. Am I? I was your...I was your night of passion." She held her hands up in quotation marks.

I carefully eyed our surroundings. Bowen stood watch at the

end of the hall out of earshot. Jules's escort wasn't far behind. The remaining nobles who'd been hanging on, hoping to be heard or seen as important, were busy gossiping as they headed down the hall.

"Is that what people still believe?" I asked quietly.

Jules shrugged. "No one has ever asked me anything, so it's hard to say."

Myself to Moriel. Just as well. It was a stupid, half-ass, shit plan anyway. And the fact that I'd heard no word or rumor of the engagement to Kane was meaningless. My father knew how to operate in secret when he wanted.

"Well, then was there—?" I froze, seeing long locks of luscious brown hair turn to flame beneath the sunlight streaming in through a window.

Lady Lyriana paused and looked down the hall, her eyes finding mine and making my heart stop. She glanced between me and Jules, a slight pout on her face, both eyebrows narrowed in concern, before she moved forward.

Jules turned as the hem of Lady Lyriana's gown floated out behind golden sandals that vanished around the corner.

"Lady Lyriana..." I said, my body heating. Gods, it was just a name. Just her name.

"I am Lady *Julianna*," Jules said with a smirk.

"I'm well aware. I was asking about her."

"What about her?" Jules asked innocently.

I glared. "Did anyone ever tell you that you're very annoying."

She grinned. "Only for you. I know how little you socialize, therefore I must offer you the full gamut of social interactions to keep you from becoming a complete asshole. And for the record, I'm adorable. And the darling of Bamarian parties."

"Auriel's bane. And amongst all of those qualities, do you have one that answers questions? I have to know. What does *she* think?" I asked. *What does she think happened? What does she think of me? Was she cold to me the other night because that's how we are, because I've convinced her I'm not worth bothering with? Or does she believe I had a negative interaction with you? Have I fucked everything up for no reason at all?*

Jules leaned closer to me, her eyes moving rapidly across the hall to scan for anyone watching. She was too close for what was considered proper.

"Is she still in danger?" she asked, voice low.

I shook my head, noting that Bowen had taken a protective stance, his arm muscles flexed. "I don't know," I said seriously. "I haven't heard anything. But I've been listening. I'm hoping not, or hoping it's lessened. Her, um, staying away from me was good." I think.

"Maybe then you should avoid parading around the fortress with no shirt on and your abs out on display after midnight."

I was stunned. My chest and abs had been exposed that night. I hadn't even thought about it. But then there was that brief moment her eyes had looked me up and down. I'd been so hot, and my bruises so faded... Shit.

"Did she say something to you?" I asked.

"She said, put a shirt on." Jules rolled her eyes, her lips quirking. "Are you sure about all of this? I see the way you two look at each other in Court, and dinner when you think the other won't see. Like you're both dying of thirst. I want to protect her —but...seeing the two of you not together...."

I looked up to see Lady Romula, Tristan Grey's grandmother, prancing down the hall surrounded by mages in blue robes and silver belts. She noted me with Jules and slowed down, moaning as she leaned on the nearest mage for support. "Is anyone courting her?" I asked, changing the subject.

"Lyr?" Jules narrowed her eyes. "Why? Are you ready to pursue and woo?"

"Lord Grey," I said, gritting my teeth. His grandmother had

righted herself and was deep in conversation with Lady Arianna. "He likes her."

Jules gave a small smile. "He does. He's a perfect match. And they've been friends a long time. But I believe they are discussing the possibility of him with Meera."

Of course, they were. That made sense. "But he's more interested in Lyriana. I've seen it."

"How can you tell?" she asked.

"I'm a man. I can tell."

She bit her lip. "So?"

I shrugged. "Encouraging it…." My stomach twisted. Fuck. I did not like that man. I did not like his family. They hunted vorakh. They'd hunt me if given the chance. My father would probably love that. He'd pay them, set up a hunt for fun. But awful personality aside, securing Lady Lyriana a marriage in Bamaria was a good way to ensure no other offers came in or demands were made. "Encouraging it might be to her benefit. Especially if…if she returns his affections." I hated the idea of her trapped in a marriage she didn't want, whether it was in the north or the south.

"I didn't take you for one to play matchmaker," Jules said.

"I'm not."

"I also didn't take you for a fan of Tristan's."

I practically growled in response.

She huffed out a breath. "Rhyan, I can help if you let me. If you tell me what's actually going on. I want to help."

Bowen began to approach.

"My time here is up," I said and reached forward for her hand, pressing a kiss to the back of it. "Thank you for speaking with me, Lady Julianna."

She curtseyed. "Your grace." She began to turn then stopped. "Will we see you? Tomorrow night at the solstice celebration?"

"I'm not one for celebrations."

She dropped her mouth open as if in surprise. "No! You? I'm shocked! Come on. We'll have mead. Your favorite."

I glared.

"The night's going to pass anyway. Might as well pass beneath the stars with a drink in your hand as musicians play."

"My lady," I said in dismissal and turned on my heels, marching back to my room with Bowen in my shadow.

CHAPTER
SEVEN

The day of the solstice felt the same as any other—long. Despite my desire to see Lady Lyriana more and despite Jules's friendly invitation, I had planned to spend the entire day and night in isolation. Luckily, the events of the day set me up for just that.

Most of Arkasva Batavia's Court had abandoned Cresthaven and its grounds for the day to attend celebrations across Bamaria. They appeared at the Temple of Dawn, and from what I'd gathered, made separate and brief appearances in Urtavia, the main city of Bamaria. As a rule, Arkasva Batavia kept public appearances to a minimum since he'd been attacked by a mob in the city after he'd taken the Seat.

I used my newfound freedom to wander the halls unseen and unbothered, without anyone staring at me or scurrying to the side to avoid my presence. I ventured down to the beach Lady Lyriana seemed to love and let the waves rush against my bare feet. I even did some laps in the pools, working off some of the tension I'd felt all morning after a heated exchange with my father.

He'd left, along with most of his men, to attend the city celebrations.

As the longest day of the year came to a close, despite the sun still blasting, I heard a commotion outside the fortress walls. I'd taken my scroll to the pool, finding it was nice to read in the warm weather when Lord Grey wasn't prowling the grounds to find Lady Lyriana.

A horn blared, and yells and shouts filled the outer fortress walls. What had felt like a calm, deserted palace transformed in seconds to a frenzy of guards and servants racing back and forth, taking up their posts, and cleaning. I slid from the edge of the pool, rerolling my scroll and sliding it back into its leather case across my shoulder.

Half a dozen seraphim birds, their blue carriages sparkling in the enduring sun, appeared beyond the gates. They opened, and Arkasva Batavia's personal guard emerged, marching forward to the promenade at a near run. Lady Meera emerged next, surrounded by soturi, and then Lady Morgana appeared with Lady Lyriana and Jules, all breaking propriety to run behind their father as sentries materialized from behind the bushes and trees —all armed.

Was Cresthaven under attack? Where was my father? What in Lumeria was going on?

A pair of boots slapped against the glass of the waterway before me.

"The fuck is going on, Bowen?" I asked.

"A surprise visit for tonight's celebration. Imperator Kormac has decided to attend unexpectedly."

I seethed. "Unexpected to whom?"

"Arkasva Batavia, of course."

I gripped the leather of my scroll's satchel between my hands. "And my father?"

Bowen shrugged, a look of derision on his face. "Imperators talk."

"And you didn't think to warn me?"

"What warning would you need? Imperator Kormac is not

your enemy."

I ran onto the waterway, racing for the entrance.

A sea of silver armor approached the gates. Imperator Kormac was here in all his glory. He looked like an arkturion leading a legion into battle.

I raced inside, finding Arkasva Batavia's sentries arranging themselves in formation to greet Imperator Kormac. My father strolled down the stairs surrounded by his guard, a victorious grin on his face, his hand lazily on the hilt of his sword.

He'd known Imperator Kormac was coming. Was this it? Was tonight the night the deal would be struck? Would there be a marriage contract? Or was some other heinous deal on the table?

I joined my father's side, my body tight with tension.

"What in Lumeria?" my father snarled as he eyed my satchel. "You should be wearing a sword not a fucking book."

"Swords are for soturi," I said evenly. "I look forward to the removal of my Birth Bind at the end of summer and earning my blade then."

My father's nostrils flared, his mouth twitching. But I'd upheld the lie he'd forced me to carry all these months.

"If you make it to the end of summer."

The sentries stood at attention, and Imperator Kormac marched through the double doors, the Bastardmaker on one side and his horrid excuse for a son, Viktor, on the other. Viktor had the same black eyes as his father and the Bastardmaker, a constant scowl on his spoiled face, and an entitled way of walking that made me nauseated. I'd been forced to endure far too many dinners and formal occasions with the bratty, insolent rodent. Gods help everyone when he was of age. When he became a soturion, he'd be a monster. Already, he was offering a lascivious leer to the noblewomen in the room.

Imperator Kormac stalked forward, and the tiniest gasp of horror escaped from down the row. Lady Julianna.

As a member of Ka Batavia but not an heir in line to the

Seat, she'd been relegated to the side and stood one ancient mage away from me. The color drained from her face as she watched him. I carefully eyed our surroundings and was sure I could offer her a hand to squeeze without anyone noticing. I extended my arm behind the mage's flowing blue robes until my fingers brushed against her arm, hitting a cool golden cuff in the shape of seraphim feathers.

She turned toward me, eyes wide, her hair still looking a little too wild for the formal greeting of an Imperator.

She raised her eyebrows, her mouth opened with a question. *What?*

Are you okay? I mouthed.

Her nostrils flared, her eyebrows narrowing in response. I moved my hand down to find hers and wrapped my fingers around her palm. I offered one squeeze, one reassuring touch, that said I was there, too; she wasn't alone. Then I retreated before anyone could see.

Jules frowned then seemed to remember who she was, where she was, and who stood before her. She donned the mask of a beautiful and proper noble. She curtseyed to Imperator Kormac and smiled sweetly as he took her hand, the one I'd just held. The southern Imperator pressed a kiss to the back of her palm. He moved on quickly, heading for my father, and I caught her look my way and mouth, *Thank you*, before resuming her proper stance as a lady.

I turned my attention to the two Imperators beside me, noting the familiarity that seemed to pepper the competition that brewed beneath the surface of their every interaction.

The question was—if he was back, was this mad plan of my father's also back in action? Or had it never been on pause and I was the idiot left in the dark?

Only one way to find out. It was settled. Tonight, I'd be attending the Bamarian summer solstice celebration.

When the formalities of the greeting were complete, I

retreated to my room to bathe and dig into my wardrobe for my formal tunic, belt, and sandals. I hadn't worn them since the day we'd arrived, and to my surprise, they all felt tight. I fit into clothes, but the belt needed to be loosened, and the tunic hugged my muscles in a way it hadn't before. Mainly because it was hugging muscles that I wasn't entirely sure had been there the last time I wore them.

Most soturi grew in size, stature, and muscle almost instantly after their Birth Bind was released. I flexed an arm in the mirror, testing, and nearly stumbled back when a bulge emerged that had definitely not been that size before. I couldn't attribute any of this to working out or training. Sure, I took walks, had made a few night visits to the Katurium to run on their track. I did push-ups in my room when the itching made me want to go insane. But none of that explained the changes I was seeing.

Either my body was rejecting the Bind, or something else was happening. I was bigger than I had been when I arrived. Perhaps I was stronger, too. What else hadn't I considered?

If Uncle Sean could see me now.

Can you imagine a rope holding this one down? That would be the lame joke he'd make. But then again, I was bound by invisible rope, and it didn't seem to be holding me any longer....

I adjusted the tunic once more to make sure it hung loosely enough over my thighs. It should have covered my knees, but the hem now sat just above them.

It would have to do until I could be refitted. There seemed little point in that before I was fully unbound and partaking in soturion training. I was fairly certain I'd grow even more at that point.

Because Bamarians considered this part of the festivities an after-party, the affair was much more casual than what the nobles of Ka Batavia had attended during the day. When I was ready, I was able to catch a seraphim carriage on my own—along with Bowen and two more members of my father's guard.

We landed in the green fields beside Bamaria's temple, the sun only just beginning to fade. The entire area was full of golden suntrees, their leaves all glowing and alight. Several small bonfires were lit, creating a sort of enclosure for the festivities. Plates of food and glasses of wine floated on trays overhead as mages extended their staves to retrieve whichever treats they wanted.

As a bound Lumerian and one who'd be becoming a soturion, I had no such ability to feed myself, so I made my way over to the food and drink stands where I was greeted with a tall glass of exactly what I wanted.

I planned to keep my wits about me, so I also made myself a plate of food. But because this was after dinner, the majority of the presentation involved desserts. I spotted several rows of tiny lemon cakes, each dripping in glaze. They'd been cut into mini-suns.

I placed one on my plate, wondering if Lady Lyriana would do the same when she made her way over.

Beside the cakes were pistachio cookies shaped like stars. The shaved nuts over the center were golden. I swiped several of those as well and shoved them at Bowen to hold while I assessed the festivities.

"Lord Rhyan," said Jules offering me a formal curtsey. "You came."

I nodded. "As you said, the time was going to pass anyway."

Jules groaned. "Ugh. I have a feeling you'd be a lot of fun to hang out with if you stopped being so committed to misery all the time."

"You haven't met many northerners then. We take our commitments very seriously."

She laughed. "You're impossible. Also...thank you. Again. For earlier."

"No need." I nodded again, looking out at the crowd. I recognized Lady Arianna and her blonde-haired daughter arriving.

Lord Grey was close by with his ridiculous-looking entourage of mages following his every move. Plenty of Soturi of Ka Batavia were on guard on the edges of the field, but every few feet or so, partygoers wearing flowing, bright dresses and tunics were interrupted by soturi in silver, wolf-pelted armor. Ka Kormac.

Imperator Kormac had to be nearby.

As did my father, based on the number of soturi in black leather I recognized as members of his guard. The Soturi of Ka Kormac and the Soturi of Ka Hart with their wolf and gryphon sigils were definitely outnumbering the golden-armored Soturi of Ka Batavia. Not a good sign.

"Are you looking for her?" Jules asked.

I glared at Jules. "You have a way about you where you change the subject with questions that make no sense nor have anything to do with the current conversation."

"Mmmhmmm," she said dismissively. "Last time you called that me 'being too perceptive for my own good.'"

"Yes, well tonight it's just annoying."

"Haha," she said, voice droll. "But in case you were wondering—which I know you are even if you won't admit it—she's heading over to us right now."

I turned in the direction Jules was pointing, and sure enough, Lady Lyriana was walking across the field in a long white dress. It seemed to be made of one long piece of fabric—almost like a soturion cloak. She'd actually styled it as one. The white fabric was pleated around her waist and secured with a golden belt, then wrapped around her torso in an X to cover her breasts, revealing the expanse of her belly below. The remaining material flared out behind her like a cape. The idea of her as a soturion, running across a battlefield and wielding a sword, seeing the muscles of her legs work...I was glad in that moment my tunic still had some spare room below the belt.

The sky darkened as she moved closer, but I was sure this

time it wasn't my eyes playing tricks on me and actually because it was finally late enough for the sky to dim with sunset.

Lyriana looked luminous, the waning sunshine not quite hitting her hair, so it remained a deep, luscious brown falling in loose waves across her shoulders.

"Lord Rhyan, your grace," she said, her eyes alight with hints of gold.

"Lady Lyriana," I said and bowed my head.

"I didn't think you were coming tonight," she said evenly.

Jules laughed. "I'm training him to have fun."

My eyes caught Lyriana's, a slight frown on her lips before she turned back to her cousin.

Jules grabbed her around the waist and pulled her close. "Ready to dance?"

Lady Lyriana seemed to relax at this and playfully shimmied her hips. "Always." She reached out a hand, the golden bangles at her wrist chiming with the beads and charms attached to them. A glass floated toward her, and her fingers grasped the stem. "What are you having?" she asked Jules.

Jules gave me a sly grin. "Lord Rhyan's favorite. Mead."

"Same then," Lady Lyriana said, glancing toward me then back to her cousin. She was standing close enough that I could smell a hint of her perfume—sweet and musky, like spiced vanilla. It was the best thing I'd ever smelled, and I wanted to get closer to her, inhale her.

"Let's toast," Jules announced as a bottle of mead floated over and poured itself into Lady Lyriana's glass.

I coughed nervously, knowing I was playing with fire standing so close to her. But then Lady Morgana and Lady Meera joined our circle.

"Your grace," Lady Meera said politely. "Are we toasting?" she asked Jules.

"I'm not sure you can call it toasting when you're drinking water," Jules teased.

"I'm not sure you can call it toasting when it doesn't involve toast," Meera said.

"Can we stop?" Lady Morgana said, holding out her glass. "Fill mine up."

The mead bottle flowed over Lady Morgana's hand, and soon all the Heirs of Ka Batavia and Jules had a full glass in hand whether it was of mead or water.

"And now, we shall toast," Lady Meera said formally.

At once we all clinked our glasses together.

"*Rapatayim!*" we shouted and sipped.

Lady Lyriana downed nearly half her glass before she grinned and yelled, "To your feet!" She threw one arm in the air, and twirled in a circle, and fuck I couldn't take my eyes off of her.

"Auriel's bane, Lyr," Lady Morgana groaned. "Every fucking time!"

Lady Meera rolled her eyes, primly sipping her water, but Jules had slammed her hand against her face, bursting into a round of helpless giggles alongside Lady Lyriana.

I wanted to laugh and had to stop myself.

Rapatayim was the traditional toast in Lumeria, but it literally meant "to your feet." Not contextually of course, but I'd never heard anyone translate it so exact. It was pretty Gods-damned adorable that this was the way she toasted.

Still, I schooled my face to neutral and saw Lady Lyriana was watching me, disappointment in her eyes. She had no idea what I was thinking.

My heart sank.

Good. She needed to stay away from me, to dislike me.

Lyriana quickly recovered as drums began to beat, their sound enhanced with a volumizing spell, and a series of water dancers assembled in the center of the field as the Arkmage of Bamaria walked around handing out blue ribbons for each dancer to tie around their feet.

"Are you joining the water dance?" Lady Lyriana asked her sisters.

Both Lady Meera and Lady Morgana shook their heads.

"That's your thing, Lyr," Lady Meera said. "But I'll watch and clap."

"Been there, seen that. Catch you later," Lady Morgana said as she refilled her glass. She turned to me. "Nice to see you out for once, your grace. Thought you were allergic to fun."

"I was, but I took my medicine tonight," I said, as she waved and took off, leaving me with Jules and Lady Lyriana once more.

The drums beat faster, and Jules shooed her cousin away from us. Lyriana ran forward, taking a ribbon from the Arkmage. The dance had already begun, but she was able to seamlessly integrate herself in an open spot. She didn't stay there long. Within a minute, she had moved to the center of the performance, her body undulating, hips snaking up and down, and face full of mischief and glee as she performed the "Dance of Asherah." It was all I could do to keep my mouth closed. Her skills as a water dancer and her memorization of the choreography were absolutely flawless. And the way the magic of the dance made it appear as if the ribbons were water...I was brought back to the day I saw her emerge from the ocean, the water dripping down her body, the waves like a cape behind her.

The appearance of my father pulled my attention. I turned from the dance performance and came face to face with Bowen, who was holding my untouched plate of lemon cake and pistachio cookies.

I felt self-conscious grabbing the lemon cake, like he knew what it meant, knew why I'd selected it. So I reached for the cookies and stuffed them in my mouth instead. They melted easily against my tongue, more pleasant than I'd realized, before I finished them off with what remained in my glass.

Lord Grey was bringing forward his entourage, which included a bouncy girl with hair so identical in color to his I assumed they were related. There was also another nobleman with dark skin and the sigil for Ka Scholar on his tunic.

"Your grace," Lord Grey said as he approached. He snapped his fingers, and a glass of red wine floated into his open hand.

"Lord Grey." I dipped my chin in respect.

"Lord Tristan," he said, returning a reluctant show of courtesy.

"No, I'm Lord Rhyan." I grinned in mock offense.

He cocked his head to the side, his neck turning red. It was too easy with this one. "In the south, we use a person's title followed by their first name."

"Oh, I'm well aware of that fact," I said. "The thing is, I just don't care."

"Just like you don't care for other's reputations?" he sneered, his eyes moving between me and Jules, who had pulled her gaze from Lyriana's performance to watch us.

"There's only one I'm concerned with," I said, knowing he'd think I meant myself, which was just as well.

"So you think it's all right to make a scene and take any noblewoman you want?"

"Tristan," Jules said, her voice full of warning. "He didn't *take* me."

I shook my head at her not to intervene. As if on cue, the other members of Lord Grey's escort took several steps back.

"You are a guest in Bamaria. No one gives a fuck that you're Heir to the Arkasva and Imperator of the north."

I shrugged. "I think the Arkasva and Imperator of the north gave at least one fuck. Once."

He grimaced. "You brute. I don't care how noble you are. You do not belong anywhere near the ladies of Ka Batavia."

"You should be fucking glad I was." I stepped closer. "Your precious Imperator had ill intentions for the lady you claim to be defending. But as I recall, you sat by like a useless slug and did nothing." I had no respect for men who claimed to care for others but sat by doing nothing because of propriety. Of course, there were rules of society and power structures, but to simply sit by, to look away—no. I'd risked a beating for her sake, risked my own reputation. And I'd do it again.

"You don't understand how things work here, how things work when your father isn't Imperator."

"You think that makes it any easier?" I snapped.

"I did what I could under the circumstances. I comforted and distracted Lady Lyriana from such things," Lord Grey snarled.

"Then be honest about your true concern," I said. "Hers. And not the Lady Julianna's."

"I never said Lyriana was not *my* concern." He said her name with such possession, such confidence.

My throat tightened. I felt sick. He was going to court her. And she should court him. It was smart—it would save her so much heartache. But fuck, I hated everything about this. About him. "Is that your plan then?" I asked. "To distract her the rest of her life?"

"What's it to you?" he asked.

"I'm asking the questions here," I replied coolly. "I outrank you, little lord. And I always will, as you so reminded me. My father's Imperator. And I don't feel inclined to answer any questions tonight. Only to ask them."

"Because you want her. Right, Lord Rhyan? I've seen you. I've seen the way you look at her. The way your eyes follow her every move. The lust you can barely contain."

"And I've seen yours. So go on then. Do something about it. Go talk to her." My guts twisted. I didn't want this.

"I don't take orders," Lord Grey snarled. "Not from lords of the north."

"You can only say that because we're not in the north. And I am only going to let this go and not create a scene, Lord Grey, out of respect for my host Arkasva Batavia. But if you do not take the next ten seconds to fuck the hell away from me, I may just forget my manners."

I stepped forward. I wasn't a soturion yet, but I was built like one. Even if my powers had only been unleashed for minutes, my body had clearly begun accepting the change. I'd always been tall, always bigger than others, always looked like I could take a punch in a fight. I'd never hit anyone before, never even tested my strength before accidentally throwing Sean across the beach, but I was becoming very curious about what it might feel like to unleash myself now. And to do so on Lord fucking Grey.

"Tristan, come on," said the bouncy girl. "It's not worth it. We're supposed to be having fun tonight."

"Come on, man," said the man from Ka Scholar. "Let's go."

I watched Lord Grey's nostrils flare, the absolute inability of his pride to allow him to concede. But then the other Ka Batavia cousin, Lady Naria, snuck her way into the group. She looked doe-eyed at Lord Grey before offering what I assumed was meant to be a seductive smile. Lord Grey's eyes instantly fell on her breasts. Smaller than Lady Lyriana's, but…still breasts.

"My lady," he said. "I've been meaning to talk to you."

I rolled my eyes.

Lady Naria looked thrilled. "I've been wanting to talk to you all day, my lord."

"I'm here, too," Jules said pointedly at her cousin.

Lady Naria glanced back with disdain. "No one said you weren't. Did you expect me to bow? Because you live in the main keep? You won't get one from me. You're not one of them, Jules."

"A simple hello would have sufficed. Auriel's fucking bane." Jules rolled her eyes. "Just go."

"Come, Naria." Lord Grey wrapped his arm around her, his hand dangerously close to the curve of her ass, which Lady Naria didn't seem to mind one bit.

I could have sworn we were about to come to blows over

Lady Lyriana just seconds ago. Were we not fighting about her? Had that just been a regular old pissing match? What a fucking waste of time.

They walked off, moving away from their friends though several of Lord Grey's mages kept following in the shadows. They walked past the water dancers, and that was when I knew. I was right. Lord Grey stopped dead in his tracks and watched Lady Lyriana stomp her feet, her hips shimmying so fast she seemed inhuman, powerful, ethereal—like a goddess. The movement exposed the soft expanse of her leg, her thigh thick and muscled with a golden chain around it. I wanted to slide my hand beneath that chain, touch her skin. Touch her. I pulled my gaze up, mesmerized. Lyriana was just so stunning.

She turned in a circle, her hips lifting and dropping so precisely in tune to the drums I swore she controlled them. She spun again, the dancers behind her following, barreling into a dizzying speed until Lyriana came to a sudden stop, a drop of sweat sliding between her breasts, her skin glowing with exertion.

Lord Grey was glued to the performance and only moved along when the drums reached a second crescendo. Lady Naria grabbed his hand, dragging him away.

Lyriana shimmied again, the drums beating faster and faster as she twirled and stomped and moved forward, a delighted yet determined expression on her face.

Gods, I could have watched her dance all night, watched her dance for days and never tired of it. But the song ended. The dancers cheered and hugged as the crowd applauded and sang their praise. I noticed the wolves of Ka Kormac looking rather annoyed. They'd ogled the dancers openly but now seemed angry as the dancers dispersed and slid off their ribbons, some discarding them, some tying them around their wrists or into their hair.

Lady Julianna made a small noise of farewell and rushed into the center of the field to join Lyriana. Lady Meera and Lady Morgana were also there laughing and giggling. Another song began, and Lyriana began to dance informally with her family, her blue ribbon tied like a bow around her wrist.

I stayed by the desserts, refilling my glass and occasionally nibbling on a pistachio cookie as more songs played and the field filled with more Lumerians celebrating and drinking. The sun finally took its leave, allowing for a star-filled sky to reign in its stead.

Realizing I was beginning to look out of place, I moved through the celebration, Bowen shadowing me, my father's men lurking in the shadows. I tried to become invisible as I found myself nearer the Soturi of Ka Kormac, hoping one would slip and tell me why they were here, what they knew.

But I couldn't get anything beyond some crude comments.

Some pompous-ass lesser noble I didn't recognize from Court had had the audacity to sneak into Lyriana's circle and had taken her hand, twirling her into a dance. He playfully untied her blue ribbon and tied it around his head. My hands flexed at my side, curling into fists with the sudden feeling that I had to go in there, rip that ribbon from him and take what was mine.

But that wasn't my place. And she wasn't mine. She never had been. She never would be.

Then I spotted him, my fucking father, standing beside the Imperator of the south. They wore identical black arkasvim robes bordered in gold, sandals shined to perfection, and the self-assured lazy smiles of men who held absolute power and had never once been held accountable for their actions.

My father leaned in toward Imperator Kormac and lifted his hand, his finger pointing right at Lady Lyriana. Imperator Kormac nodded with a wolfish grin then gestured for my father to follow. They began to retreat from the festivities, their personal guards shifting position, black leather and silver metal moving as one.

I moved forward, sliding in and out of the crowd, trying to avoid being seen. This would have been a handy time to have a soturion cloak—I could have vanished. I supposed my vorakh would have suited me just as well.

But as I ventured closer, I lost sight of them completely. The trees were so tightly knit together here. All I found were several soturi shooting me warning glances to turn around. I shifted my angle, trying to listen. Hearing hushed voices, I stepped forward slowly, heading further into the darkness, broken only by hanging twinkling lights in the trees. The whispers grew louder and transformed into a groan of pleasure.

I froze. The moan intensified, and I decided to retreat. It couldn't be my father—not with Imperator Kormac...I didn't think. But if it was, they'd kill me if I knew.

I turned back, trying to find my way out of the wood, when I stumbled upon the source of the moans and groans.

Lord Grey. He leaned against a suntree, his hands fisted into a head of blonde hair, the girl's dress falling off her shoulders, leaving her upper back exposed as her hand clearly worked between his legs.

Lady Naria.

I stepped back, but it was too late. Lord Grey's eyes fell on me. He stilled, looking panicked, his neck red and strained as he tried to still Naria and cover himself. I stared back, my lips curling into a sneer, my nostrils flaring before I turned. I was done. I didn't need to see any more of this, and I wasn't likely to find my father and Imperator Kormac. If they truly were plotting, both were intelligent enough to retreat to a secure location.

Unlike Lord Fucking Grey, who had his designs on Lady Lyriana but thought it was perfectly all right to kiss and whatever else was about to happen with her cousin where anyone could see.

I headed back toward the noise of the crowd, the beating of

the drums. An opening lay ahead, bonfires roaring in the distance.

"Come now, you're acting so very foolish," said a voice that left me cold. It was familiar to me now. Ethereal. Musical. The voice of an Afeya. The same one I'd seen in the Great Library, on the beach. The same one who'd spoken into my mind. "Lady Lyriana Batavia, as she is currently known, is not ready."

"We need to plant seeds, or she will fail as Lyriana," said a second voice, this one female with a heavy accent. She shifted her position, sending out the sound of ringing seashells. She wore the same odd dress as before, her hair nearly purple in the moonlight.

By the Gods. This was the third time I'd spotted Afeya watching Lyriana. The hell did they want from her?

"The seeds are planted. I dug through the earth to create the holes myself. Do not act without me," seethed the male. "My plan has been in place for a millennium, and yet you underestimate me. Me!"

"I wouldn't, but this plan moves too slow. And what about him?" asked the female. "He's here now. Getting closer to her. Too close."

Him?

"Exactly," he purred. "Exactly where I want him. Leave him to me. I know what to do." The Afeya stepped forward. "Go home. Aren't they missing you in El Zandria?"

"You're not missed in the Night Lands?"

Afeyan countries. My heart pounded.

"Your daughter is working very well with me," said the male. "In case you wanted to feign interest."

"My daughter's wasting away in the library."

The male Afeya shook his head. "She's too smart to tell you her true mission. Enough. We're here tonight. And there she is. Holding the name Lyriana," he laughed, saying her name oddly like he wasn't taking her seriously, "she does look delicious. And oh so alone," he purred. "I believe the next dance will require a partner. She needs a dance partner. I could fulfill that need for her."

He was going to approach her. Dance with her. Make a deal. Or worse.

"Lucky, you have plenty of time to decide. Not millennium. But this droll song only lasts another several minutes," snapped the female Afeya.

"I could end it now if I so desired," he said, his voice full of mischief.

My heart raced. The Afeya snapped his fingers, and the drums stopped. There were several surprised yells from the crowd, from Lumerians who'd been dancing. Musicians who'd looked stunned, shaking out their instruments, or blowing silently into their horns and flutes. But within seconds the instruments began to sound again as a slower song played—the lover's dance, the music of Auriel and Asherah.

"Quick enough for you?" asked the male Afeya.

I inched forward, sensing Bowen not far behind. Beyond me was the festival, full of Lumerians looking perplexed at the sudden change in music, but still rushing to pair off. Couples were forming across the dance floor, and standing in the center, her dress of white glowing in the moonlight, was Lady Lyriana. Alone.

The Afeya started forward, heading right for her. I had no idea what either Afeya had been talking about, the seeds or whatever, or which *him* they referred to. Nothing they'd said made any sense. But I knew this much—he had targeted Lady Lyriana, had been targeting her for weeks, if not longer. Whatever this plan was that involved a millennium, I wanted her nowhere near it. Nowhere near him. He was a threat, and seemed to be using magic on his own—something Afeya were supposedly unable to do. He'd even changed the music to dance with her.

I hadn't spent all summer staying away, protecting her from

my father, only to watch her come to harm by immortals. Both Imperators were still deep in the woods; my father wouldn't see me go to her. I prayed he stayed there long enough for me to succeed.

The Afeya moved faster, pushing tree branches out of his way and stepping forward. I stopped thinking. I started running, weaving through the trees, the bonfires, the crowd of couples. I didn't stop. Not until I was before her.

The Afeya didn't dare step onto the dance floor. I wasn't entirely sure he was welcome in Bamaria at the moment—or visiting legally. Afeya had to make themselves known to the council of each country immediately upon entry and were often escorted by council members at all times. Though many went rogue. This one was not here by invitation since he kept to the shadows. But I could see him clearly, his violet eyes on me, his lips curled in anger as he moved through the edge of the celebration, vanishing and reappearing in the trees. The diamonds on his body reflecting in the bushes.

I raced past a tightly knit crowd of Lumerians blocking my way to Lyriana. She was on the edge of the dance floor, so close to the woods—so close to a place where the Afeya could lure her to him. And then he was there—the female now beside him, her seashells chiming, the sound ringing in my head. I pushed through a couple, roughly separating them. The Afeya had taken one step onto the dance floor, the second following close. And then I was before Lyriana, scrambling to get my bearings and coming into an awkward stop as her attention was pulled to the side. Toward the spot where the Afeya stood. Quickly, I straightened my tunic, pushing back my hair as I stepped into her line of sight, just beating out the Afeya's next step.

"Your grace," Lady Lyriana said.

"Lady Lyriana," I said, offering a curt bow. I wanted to apologize to her for being rude earlier—for being rude all summer. But I didn't have time. I had to become her dance partner right then. No Afeya would interfere directly, publicly with two heirs to the Arkasva. Not when one was the son of an Imperator.

The Afeya moved aside, still hiding between the trees, staring right at me, something feral and vicious in his expression. His blue skin was darkening, his spiral tattoos seeming to come to life, spinning into tiny glittering diamonds across his nearly naked body.

"Take my hand," I said.

Her eyes widened. "What?"

I held out my hand, my feet assuming the dance position required. "Take my hand."

Her eyes searched mine. I could see the hesitation in them.

"Dance with me," I said. "Please."

She nodded, and then, at last, her hand touched mine, warm and soft. Our fingers threaded together, naturally, like they were used to touching, as I stepped into her space. I slid my free hand across her waist as my stomach tightened, throat dry, and I pulled her close.

I was dancing with Lyriana.

CHAPTER
EIGHT

We moved through the first few steps in silence. My body brimming with tension and my heart racing as I scanned the field, watching both Afeya retreat into the trees, their bodies vanishing into the dark.

How many Lumerians and Afeya were plotting against Lady Lyriana? She wasn't even Heir Apparent. What did they know about her that I didn't? That perhaps even she didn't yet know?

I stared over her shoulder, feeling dread at the thought of who might see us. I'd been brash. But the Afeya had named her, had used magic to approach her and come so close. Too close. I couldn't stand back and do nothing. And I knew my father was still deep in the woods conspiring, but we were still in public. Anyone could be reporting my every move to him just like they did back home.

"You seem distracted," Lady Lyriana said.

"What?" I asked then realized I'd missed a step. I spun her around and pulled her back in, this time with my gaze focused solely—and helplessly—on her. "Better?" I asked.

She shrugged, looking uncomfortable. "It's all right. You don't have to dance with me."

"Do you not want to dance with me?" I blurted out.

"No, I mean, I don't not want to, but I…. Do you not want to dance with me?" she asked.

Gods, I'd muddied everything between us this summer. I leaned closer to her as wind blew against her back, pushing her hair forward, carrying the scent of her perfume—a musky vanilla—from her skin toward me. Yes, I had my reasons for approaching her, but given the chance, given the option to dance with her, I'd always say yes. And perhaps the Afeya had been just an excuse.

I exhaled, knowing they were gone, and stared into Lyriana's hazel eyes. "I asked you to dance with me, Lady Lyriana. If I hadn't wanted to dance with you—I wouldn't be here now. I swear."

Her eyes widened, that same defensiveness in them I'd seen all those years ago when I'd interrogated her about what she was reading.

I was an ass. A worthless piece of gryphon-shit who should have been walking away. I searched her eyes, trying to decide what to do.

"Unless…. Are you uncomfortable with me?" I loosened my grip on her hand immediately. "I'll go."

She shook her head. "No. Don't. I just…." She sighed. "All summer, I thought you hated me."

I laughed nervously, feeling her push back, but this time I pulled her closer. "Quite the opposite." I glanced over her head, eyeing the soturi in the field, some with silver armor and others with black leather armor adorned with gryphons. No sign of either Imperator. No sign of either Afeya.

"But you—" she started and cut herself off.

I pulled back, staring into her eyes, my gut clenching.

"Never mind," she said, her cheeks blooming with pink.

I could end this now. Step away from her, watch from the distance to make sure no one approached. Maybe find Jules, tell her to dance with Lyriana. But now that I was here, now that she was in my arms, now that my hands were tingling from touching her, feeling the softness of her skin, the warmth of her body, and drowning in her scent, it was going to be impossible to let her go.

So, instead I said, "But I've been cold and brutish and generally unpleasant and rude since I arrived." I winked. "Honestly, if I were in your shoes, I'd think I'd hated me, too."

That earned me a smile. A gorgeous one. "Well, at least you're self-aware."

"Ouch," I said in mock hurt, placing one hand on my heart.

She laughed, the most beautiful laugh I'd ever heard. I replaced my hand on her waist, leading her into the next step.

"Self-aware's an insult in the north?" she asked.

I wrinkled my nose. "Depends who you ask. It doesn't offend me."

She raised an eyebrow in question. "Then what part of my words caused you pain, your grace?"

"Oh, well, I was hoping you'd say I was handsome, dashing, and clever. Basically, all things an Heir to the Arkasva is meant to be."

Lady Lyriana bit her lip. "I'm an Heir to the Arkasva."

I tugged her closer. "And you are extremely handsome, dashing, and clever."

She laughed again.

I turned her in my arms, circling her around me, loving the way she moved, the way she danced, the way she felt and smelled. But I also used the move to search again for anyone watching us.

But there was only one set of eyes focused our way now. Lord Grey's.

"Is this the mead making you nice?" she asked.

"The mead only makes me meaner," I said conspiratorially.

"Mystery then."

"Indeed."

"Well, whatever this is," she said shyly, "I like this side of you."

I turned her away and pulled her back into my arms. "Do you now?"

"I do," she said, her voice a hushed whisper.

We continued to dance, our feet stepping easily in sync, our hips swaying as stars sparkled in the sky above. More couples joined the dance floor, surrounding us, circling around us. Each new dancer seemingly had eyes only for their dance partner and them alone.

It felt like we were being swallowed up, existing in a place that was just for us, where no one could see us and no enemies could interfere.

The notes of the lover's danced swelled, and I caught Lyriana's eye, my heart pounding. She was so bright, so luminous, the stars which had twinkled overhead just seconds ago dimmed, and all at once, my chest tightened.

For him, she's brighter than the brightest star in Heaven.

Words from the Valya, words to describe how Auriel fell in love with the Goddess Asherah.

I swallowed, my throat feeling dry. No. That wasn't possible. I barely knew her. I was just attracted to her, and...felt safe with her. And wanted to protect her. And talk to her. Ask her about the Guardian, read scrolls together on a lazy afternoon, share cake...kiss... But I wasn't...I wasn't sure I was capable of feeling love. Or anything close to it.

Feelings were far too dangerous things to have in my world. They made you weak. They gave your enemies something to take, something with which to hurt you. They became nightmares that left you waking in a cold sweat. And they became toys for your father when your body went numb from too much pain.

Lyriana moved closer. Our bodies were nearly flush against each other, my heart beating too loud, her scent everywhere.

"Are you enjoying solstice?" I asked her, trying to keep my arousal from pressing against her, from scaring her.

She stared up at me, an almost stunned expression in her eyes before she nodded. "It…it might be the best one yet."

I smiled, barely daring to believe I had anything to do with it and far too afraid to ask.

By the Gods, I was farther than Lethea. I was supposed to be staying away from her, making her hate me, protecting her, but somehow…somehow doing just that had driven me into her arms, had me holding her hands and waist while I spun her across the dance floor.

The lover's dance slowed, the music swelling into a romantic crescendo. Gods, she was so fucking beautiful. I leaned in, inhaling her scent until I was dizzy, my eyes on her lips, on the soft pink color, on the—

She gasped and stiffened.

"What's wrong?" I asked.

Lyriana stared down. "Nothing. Sorry."

"Did I do something?" I tried to straighten myself, pull back. She blushed.

"Lyriana," I said, and her eyes snapped to me. "It's all right. Whatever it is, you can tell me."

"You called me Lyriana."

Shit. Shit. I'd been so wrapped up in her, and so turned on, I'd forgotten to properly address her. "Sorry. Was that okay?"

"Only if I can call you Rhyan."

I nodded, loving the way my name sounded on her lips, loving hearing my name, just my name. No title. No connection to my father or Ka. "Please do."

"It's…." She smiled and shook her head. "It's stupid. For a second I thought…" She stared up, her cheeks round and red. "I thought you were going to kiss me."

My palm pressed against hers, and a shiver ran down my spine. Heat moved low in my belly, my cock stirring further.

"I wasn't going to kiss you," I said seriously.

She nodded, a small frown on her lips.

"I wouldn't let our first kiss be in public." I leaned in again, inhaling her scent. I'd take her somewhere private, somewhere I could have her all to myself. "But the thought of kissing you, that crossed my mind. Many times."

Our fingers were entwined, and I swore she moved closer to me, but we continued to follow the steps, swaying and spinning with the beat.

She looked away, an embarrassed smile on her lips.

The drums and lyres began to slow, the song and our dance coming to an end. It was just as well because emerging from the trees on the other side of the field were my father and Imperator Kormac. Gods. This was it. I had to leave her.

"Lyriana," I said urgently. "This was—thank you. But I have to go. Right now."

"I'll come with you," she said.

I started to shake my head, but she had this look of determination in her eyes and…something else. Something I couldn't put a name to or say no to. Like she belonged at my side.

"You sure?" I asked, already searching the crowd for Jules, her sisters, for Lord Grey even.

"Yes."

It was going to take longer to say goodbye to her than it would for her to run by my side before we were seen, and I didn't know where the Afeya were or how determined they were —at least those were the excuses I provided myself as I nodded.

I released our dance hold, taking her opposite hand in my own, our fingers threading together, my palm, warm and tingling with her touch. My father was still far from us, the dancers obscuring most of his view.

"Ready?" I asked. "I move fast. Don't let go."

"I won't."

Then we ran, racing through the remaining couples and standing soturi before disappearing into the trees, away from my father, away from the party. We moved into such a deep part of the woods, it felt like we'd even moved away from the stars. Still, the path was clear, visible from the twinkling lights strewn across each of the golden suntrees surrounding us.

I slowed, releasing her hand, and she clutched at her chest, catching her breath.

"You really do run fast," she said, still breathing heavily. "Well, of course, you're a soturion."

I bit the inner corner of my cheek. "Not yet. Not officially."

Had she thought I was running particularly fast because more of my strength was escaping, or was she just not used to running? Most nobles weren't, particularly if they were on track to become a mage, which she and all of her bloodline had been for years.

"I didn't think...." she trailed off and smiled, shaking her head. "I didn't think this is where the night would end."

"It's not over yet," I said. "Anything could happen." I thought of Uncle Sean telling me to be open to possibilities.

Maybe anything for her was possible. If my father stayed away from her.

The music of the festival faded, and in its place came the shouting of the clock tower by Bamaria's timekeeper. I scanned around us, making sure we were alone. No soturi. No Afeya.

"Oh," Lyriana said pulling my gaze back to her, "there's an opening in the trees here." She pointed up. "You can see all the ashvan race by. At night, the blue from their magic glows brightest."

I peered up through the opening, but it was just empty sky. I frowned.

"No, wrong angle," she said. "Come here. You have to stand next to me."

Tentatively, I moved forward, leaning back against the trunk of the suntree, so aware of her presence, of her scent mixing with the fresh scent of the woods, of the sound of her breathing.

"We don't use them like this at home. The gryphons do patrol. So, I forget sometimes how beautiful their lights are. I never really see them like this at night."

Lyriana's eyes followed the movement of the blue orbs appearing and vanishing across the sky. "I forget, too," she said. "But for the opposite reason. I think it's like, when you see something all the time, you become numb to it, you know? Like, you stop noticing, stop appreciating. I like that I'm seeing them here with you. I feel like, like I'm seeing them for the first time now. Imagining them through your eyes."

I wasn't watching the ashvan anymore. Only her. The curve of her cheek, the swell of her lips, the waves of her hair falling down her back and shoulders. The long slender slope of her neck that led into her collarbone. And below that, the tantalizingly round curves I'd been trying so hard to ignore all summer.

"I know what you mean." But I was pretty sure if I saw Lyriana every day, I'd never tire to her beauty.

She sighed, and by the Gods, it was the sweetest sound I'd ever heard. Her breasts rose and fell, so Godsdamned pretty, so...I swallowed and forced my attention back to the lights.

"That must be nice," I said, watching the horses go by. Racing across the sky with such ease and confidence.

"What?" she asked, her voice low and intimate.

"Being an ashvan," I said with a laugh. "Every step you take, magic appears and supports you. I wish I knew what that was like. To always be supported when you did something. To know you couldn't fall, couldn't fail."

She turned her gaze from the ashvan to me, her eyes hooded but thoughtful before she stared back up at the sky through the trees. "I never thought of it that way." Her expression turned wistful, and she sighed again. "I want that."

"To race across the sky? Or be supported?" I asked.

"Both. But mainly supported so I can...I don't know. I just want that. I want," she turned her head, "I want more."

"More what?" I asked, unable to help myself from leaning closer. Our faces were so close. Too close. Her breath a soft wind against my hair.

"Everything." Her lips quirked into a smile, but she seemed sad as she spoke.

I nodded, urging her to go on.

"I don't usually talk about this."

"I won't tell anyone," I promised.

Her eyes searched mine, the golden flecks sparkling beneath the twinkling lights of the trees. "It's just...do you ever feel as if your entire life has been laid out before you, like there's a plan in place, a destiny with its road already paved out, only...it's just... not what you want? But you have to take a step, you can't stay still, and yet, there's no other path to take. No road leading elsewhere."

"More than you know."

She frowned. "But you're Heir Apparent."

"Exactly. The more titles behind your name, the less choices it seems you have." My hands flexed at my side, the desire to touch her coursing through me with such power, I felt like it would knock me over any second. "But," I said, thinking of Sean's words again, "I don't think that means that possibility doesn't exist. Maybe you can't see there's another path because it hasn't presented itself yet. Maybe it will when the time is right."

She considered, her expression somewhere between excitement and worry. "I hope you're right."

"Was this something you were considering that night in the Great Hall?"

Lyriana pushed some loose waves behind her ears. "I think about that a lot." She bit her lip. "The first day you were here, I thought you were...I don't know. It's stupid. But I was offended when you said I'd be a good librarian."

"That was a compliment. A high one."

She nodded. "But like I said, it's expected that I'll go into education or something like it. And I love it. I really do. But... path laid out." She gestured helplessly. "I didn't choose it." She bit her lip. "I've never told anyone before."

I was honored. "Not even Jules?" I teased.

Her face fell. "No."

"It's okay," I said. "I won't tell her either. I promise."

"Rhyan, I know what you did for her," she said softly. "I know...I know what she's been facing, even if she won't talk to me about it. Thank you."

I sighed. "You weren't supposed to know."

"She didn't say anything. I just...I saw. I see more than she wants to believe. I've been wanting to thank you for your kindness to her. All summer." She shook her head, her nostrils flaring. "That man's a monster."

"I know."

Her body angled against the tree, turning toward me. "Why won't you let anyone see who you really are?"

"There's not much to see."

"I don't know about that."

Our eyes met, and for a moment, I started to believe, truly believe, in possibility. That this, even briefly, was possible. That, even if only for tonight, I could have this—a moment for myself, a moment with her. One thing of beauty, one moment to just be, to feel. My heart was swelling, pounding, and some feeling of— fuck...hope? Hope was actually floating inside of me.

No. I didn't feel hope. I'd trained myself to not feel it years ago. Hope was changeable, hope was fleeting, dangerous. Hope meant you needed to be on guard, because it could leave at any moment.

My mind was yelling at me to run. An inner voice warned

me not to ruin her with my presence, not to allow her to become the next thing that turned to shit with my touch.

At the same time, something was on fire in my soul, and I didn't think I could walk away from her if my life depended on it.

And yes, there it was. Beating, breathing, living inside of me. Hope.

The ashvan had long landed by now, their blue lights no longer glowing in the sky. The hour was done being called, so it was silent but for our breaths, the soft hiss of wind, the chirping of crickets, and small rustlings of animals in the woods.

I shifted my back so I was no longer against the tree. Instead, I stood right before her, like she was a magnet pulling me in. She looked so beautiful my heart ached, and my lips almost seemed to be humming in pain as if they knew what they were supposed to be doing—kissing her lips, touching her lips, tasting her lips— and they were suffering in their denial.

Our eyes met, and fuck I was hers. I'd been hers since the first moment I saw her.

"What are you thinking?" she asked, leaning back, something so open and vulnerable in her expression.

"That handsome wasn't the right word for you. That you're so fucking beautiful, I can't walk away."

Her eyes searched mine. She bit her bottom lip, and my mind stopped. "I don't want you to walk away."

"I won't."

"Stay."

"I will."

"Good." Lyriana's chest rose and fell, her breath coming short as my own felt erratic.

Neither of us moved, we were both just breathing, staring.

"Your eyes," she said, almost in wonder. "They're so green. Like emeralds. They're beautiful."

I swallowed. She was the first person to ever say anything

like that—to refer to their color like that. To call them emeralds, to say they were beautiful, not strangely green, not too green. And she was the first person to make me believe she was seeing through the color, through them, seeing me. The real me. Not the one I tried to present to the world. The one who didn't care, didn't hurt, didn't...feel. But the me inside, the one I'd tried to bury years ago. The one that felt, the one that loved, the one that...hoped.

I inched closer to her, helpless to pull myself away.

Her mouth was so pretty so luscious, so enticing, as was her scent. Her entire being. I was lost, helpless against her. I knew if I didn't walk away now, she'd consume me.

"I want to kiss you," I said. "Can I?"

Her lips parted, her eyes wide, and she nodded before saying, "Yes."

My breath came fast, nerves suddenly alive everywhere as I leaned forward, one hand against the tree, the other sliding to cup her cheek as I lowered my lips to hers.

I was gentle at first, testing. Her lips remained closed against mine as if she wasn't entirely sure what to do. Slowly, I slanted my mouth over hers, kissing the corner of her mouth, her upper lip, and then teasing the bottom before kissing it, taking her lip between mine. I pulled back, checking in with her, giving her space to move forward or change her mind.

Her hands lifted, resting on my back, fingers pressing into me as I stroked my thumb against her cheek. I stared into her eyes, taking in her soft breaths as she took in mine. Then we were kissing again, and I wasn't sure who leaned into who as her hands moved up and down my back while mine glided down her neck and shoulders.

The kiss deepened, her mouth finally opening, her tongue brushing against mine in a way that sent shivers running down my spine. She felt so good. So right. A small moan escaped me.

My fingers tangled in her hair and I kissed her deeply again and again, until she made a sound that sent fire through my veins. I pressed closer to her, closing what little space remained between our bodies.

I coaxed her tongue into my mouth, as she became more confident, leaving me breathless and wild.

"I really thought all summer you didn't like me," she said, gasping between kisses.

I was so hard. I pulled her even closer, so she could feel how much I wanted her, how untrue that statement was. "I like you."

Her chest rose and fell. "I like you, too."

"Lyr," I said, daring to use her nickname, loving the way it felt to do so, the closeness of it, the intimacy. "All summer I wanted you. I always have."

I stopped pressing my other hand against the tree and slid it down the smooth skin of her arm then down her side to her waist. I gripped her there, exactly where my hand had been when we'd danced, but my touch was no longer formal or proper. It was possessive, and I was rolling her hips toward me, no longer able to stop myself from pressing completely against her, all hard where she was soft and welcoming.

Her breasts rose, so soft, pushing into my chest, and my tongue caught hers until she let out a moan.

I nibbled her lips, loving the way she felt, the way she tasted —better than I'd imagined all summer. Her hips moved, and her body began to undulate against mine like she was seeking more contact but wasn't sure what to do or how to ask for what she wanted.

I shifted, my knee going between her legs, my hand rising up her belly, touching the soft bare skin beneath her chest before stopping just below the curves hidden behind the folds of her gown. The tips of my fingers just barely brushed the underside of her breast. A peaked nipple pressed through the fabric, and fuck, I was barely hanging onto control.

She gasped, going still.

I removed my hand, pulling back. "Sorry. Too much?" I asked.

She closed her eyes, one hand over her heart, her breath heavy and uneven, her neck flushed red. "I...." She stared up at me. "I don't know."

"It's okay. You don't have to. Do you want me to stop?" *Gods, say no. Tell me to keep going, tell me you want more.*

"No," she said. "It's just...a lot. Um." She shook her head, her cheeks pink with embarrassment. "I've never done this before."

I breathed out, my breath shaky with need as I pushed her hair behind her ear, kissing her forehead gently. "You're doing so good, Lyr. So good." I kissed her forehead again. "It's okay."

"But I...." She bit her bottom lip.

"Lyr, it's fine. If this is too intense, we can stop."

"No. I...." She swallowed. "I liked it. What you were doing. A lot. I just wasn't expecting that."

I exhaled slowly, trying to cool the fire in my veins. This was her first kiss, and I didn't want to ruin it for her. I wanted it to be perfect. I wanted it to be everything she ever wanted.

"Did you mean that?" she asked.

"Everything."

"That...I was doing good?"

I smiled. "I only give compliments when I absolutely mean it. And you are doing so very good." I pushed another stray lock of hair behind her ear, my fingers trailing down the soft, silky skin of her neck as she shivered. "But we'll slow down," I said. "You're in control."

"I am?" she asked.

I pressed my forehead against hers. "By all the Gods, in this moment, you have complete and total possession of me." I nearly groaned, pulling back to see her clearly.

"Total possession?" she asked with a smile.

I couldn't stop my own smile from spreading across my face. "Careful now. I'm a lot of responsibility."

"I'll be careful." She lifted up onto her toes, and her arms wrapped around me again, pulling me toward her. My knee remained lodged between her legs, but I stayed still, letting her control the movement, the pace, keeping my hands firmly in her hair, fingers tangled.

That swelling in my heart came again, a feeling so powerful I was afraid I would burst. She could consume me, devour me in this moment, and I wouldn't care. I'd thought I was hers before, but I'd had no idea. She owned me, had complete control over my heart, my body, my soul.

"Lyr," I said, my lips moving to her cheek, trailing kisses across her jaw to her neck. "Lyr." I sucked on her skin, felt her arms tighten around me as I trailed kisses back up to her mouth, to those lips. It was all I could do not to scoop her up, press her hard into the tree and propose right there.

She lowered her hands to my waist, pulling me closer against her, her hips undulating into mine.

"Is this all right?" she asked.

"It's more than all right," I said, my breath heavy. "You feel so good."

I was getting harder by the second. Harder than I thought possible. Fuck, she felt so right. So much better than anything else ever had. Than anyone.

Her breath seemed to shorten, and I could feel her hands loosen their grip on me, like it was becoming too intense, too quick for her again.

I pulled back, letting her catch her breath and trying to catch ahold of my own runaway emotions. If she was overwhelmed by what was physically happening, I was overwhelmed by what I was feeling. It was too much. Too fucking much, too fast.

She moaned as I softly bit her neck, licking and kissing the same spot.

And then I heard the snap of a tree branch. I stilled.

We weren't alone.

Fuck. Fuck. Myself to fucking Moriel. It was like a cold bucket of water had been poured over me.

I couldn't hurt her again. It would break my heart. And running with her to another location wouldn't work either. This had been a stolen moment, and the moment was over.

I just prayed I hadn't caused too much damage.

I pulled her into my arms, holding her as close as I could, my face buried in her neck. I inhaled her scent, her sweet, beautiful scent. Her chest was rising and falling against mine, both of our breathing erratic.

"Lyr," I whispered, my arm shaking, "we're not alone. I don't think we should be seen."

She bit her bottom lip, red and plump from kissing. "You're right."

"Can you get back to the party by yourself? I'll redirect whoever's here."

She pulled back, blinking, her lips pouting slightly, but she nodded. "Okay."

"Lyr, promise me this. Don't stop until you're back with Jules or your sisters. Okay? Don't talk to anyone who approaches you before then."

She shook her head as if my request was over the top, which it was. But she agreed.

I released her and pointed her away from the sound, away from the soturion I knew was close by—and had likely been close by this entire time.

Lyr gathered her white dress, glanced over her shoulder at me, offering me one final heart-shatteringly beautiful smile. Then she ran, vanishing into the trees.

Bowen appeared in the next second, his face grim, his hand on his soturion belt, his fingers dangerously close to his sword.

"You forgot your cookies," he growled.

He opened the pouch at his side and pulled out three of the pistachio star cookies. He stepped forward and shoved them into my open palm.

"What?" I asked, staring down at the stars. They were crumbled and broken.

"Eat," he said. "This and what just happened against that tree are probably the sweetest things you'll have for a long while."

I fisted my hand, the cookies crumbling into nothing.

"Come on, your grace. Your father wants to see you."

CHAPTER
NINE

I woke the following morning in a damp gray stone cell, above me a raised ceiling with a small barred window. Small slivers of sunlight beamed down on me. My head was pounding, and my body shivered all over as if I'd just broken a fever.

The hell was I? All I remembered was kissing Lyriana. Lyr. Her musky vanilla scent, her soft skin, the feel of her body in my arms, the taste of her lips against mine, the suntree behind her....

And then Bowen had appeared and said my father was looking for me, and someone had hit me from behind.

I lifted a hand tentatively to the back of my head, and sure enough, it was tender as fuck. My vision seemed to double everything around me—the bars of my prison cell, the walls of stone, and even Bowen. Two fucking Bowens stood outside my cell.

"Where are we?" I asked, grimacing. Talking hurt. Opening my eyes hurt. Everything hurt.

"Shadow Stronghold. Historic," Bowen said cheerfully. "Like your giant gryphon statue."

My feet hit the ground as I sat up on my cot, and I cradled my head in my hands, willing my stomach to settle. I inhaled deep and looked up slowly, seeing, thank the Gods, only one Bowen this time.

"Did you hit me?" I asked.

"Your grace."

"Did you fucking hit me?"

"I'm sorry," he said.

"My father's orders?" I asked.

"Always."

Tears burned behind my eyes. "Get out."

"Your grace, my job is to—"

"Is to knock me out whenever my father asks? You're the shittiest guard that ever existed. I hope you know that. This is what your life is! Years of training to fight and build strength, only to leave your one charge subjected to the will of a monster. You don't protect me. You hurt me. And your life is fucking meaningless if that's all you're good for."

"Rhyan." He held up his hands in surrender. More emotion in his face than I'd ever seen. "I tried."

I shook my head. "It's funny. I'm getting really Godsdamned sick of hearing people tried. Did he bind you, too? Blood oath?"

His shoulders tensed. "You know your father operates in blood oaths as easily as others trade gold."

"Then why has he never fucking put one on me?"

Bowen stepped forward, almost looking afraid. "It could kill you."

"Wouldn't that please him?"

Bowen's jaw tightened. "No, your grace. That's the last thing he wants."

I watched him carefully, true fear in his eyes. My whole life I thought he'd be happier if I were dead. And for the first time, I considered, there was a reason I was here.

Something was starting to click into a place. A barely realized thought just on the edge of my mind.

I looked around my prison cell and rolled my shoulders back.

First, I had deal with this shit. My father had pulled this sort of thing before in the prisons back home. Though the conditions there had been far worse. This was almost a luxury.

But as Bowen's words sank in, I could see this now for what it was. A scare tactic. A way to keep me under control. And it was the last time I'd let it work.

I wasn't going to be afraid of him. Not any longer. I knew him well enough to know he wasn't going to let me stay in here for long. He'd need me. Need me to be at a public appearance. Need me to look healthy. Need me to not flinch before the Bamarian Council.

Right on schedule, a door in the hall opened, and my father strode through, his Imperator cloak sweeping behind him, a blur of black and gold, his aura freezing and already stabbing at me as he emerged from the shadows. His face was stern, all hard lines against the severe cut of his hair.

Shakily, I made my way to my feet, bracing against the burning cold, against the hurricane of his aura, screeching through the bars to reach me.

I shivered, but made no move to cover as black shadows from the cell striped his face.

"You thought you could manipulate me," he asked, voice low and dangerous. "Me? You idiot. Why did you think we came here? For the fucking lemon trade? Just to see Ka Kormac do what I already knew they were doing! *She* was always the plan, always the prize. And you…insolent fool. You tried so hard to spend the summer convincing me you felt nothing for the Batavia girl. Me? As if your petty, immature little mind games could have changed or altered anything! And then, right when you think I'm distracted, you go off and take her against a tree."

"I didn't take her. I kissed her. And she wanted me, too."

My father laughed. "Just know that all of your actions were a pathetic waste of your time. You were never going to save her. Even you couldn't stick to your own Godsdamned plan. As if I could have been manipulated by you for a second!" He clicked his tongue. "Kane isn't going to like that, you know, the thought of your lips on his future wife."

"She's not going to be his wife," I said calmly. The truth began to fall into place.

"When will you get it through your thick skull? You have no say in this! You never did. You think I'd go to all that trouble just to upset you. To control you? When you're already under my thumb where I want you? When I have far easier ways of doing so?" My father jerked his chin at Bowen. "Unlock his cell."

I stepped forward, but my father shook his head. "I'm not freeing you. Not yet. I paid for another hour for you to be here. And I intend to get my money's worth while you learn your *lesson*." He walked through the cell, scrunching up his nose in disgust at the smell. "I let you play your game all summer because I wanted to see what you would do. How defiant you had become of me. How full of yourself you'd grown. It's safe to say you're still weak."

I was dizzy from standing, and my father's face went in and out of focus before I steadied myself and took a step forward. Something hot, and fiery was surging inside me, burning, itching, ready to burst free.

"I am not weak," I snarled.

He took another step forward and another, his hand fists, his arm swinging. And with a punch to my gut, I was flat on the ground.

"Well?" He stood over me. "Did you at least fuck this one?"

Fury boiled inside me, the same feeling, the same strength I'd felt that day at the beach. I'd been feeling it surge like an undercurrent since I'd stopped touching Lyr, and before I knew what I was doing, I had stood, pulled my fist back, and—with nineteen years of rage, hatred, fear, and humiliation powered up behind my hand—punched my father in the fucking face.

Pain erupted like flames across my hand and down my arm.

A look of pure terror fell across my father's face as he went flying across the cell. His back hit the bars with an eerie thud before he slid to the ground, his mouth open in shock. A small trickle of blood running down his chin.

My stomach hollowed. My heart pounding. I'd never fought back before—not once. Fear suddenly gripped me. I'd done more than just attack my father. I'd attacked my Arkasva. My Imperator.

I braced myself for his next move as he wiped the blood from his mouth and stood slowly, his back sliding up the prison bars, until he was on his feet. He walked back toward me and stopped a foot away, spitting blood onto my tunic.

I stared down in disgust, missing the moment he swung and punched me again. This time, I flew back, smacking the back of my cot, before I slid to the floor.

"Bowen," my father barked. "Get the mage in here. Now."

I crawled to my feet, using the cot to help me stand, my chest heaving with exertion, my head ready to split in two. "Are you going to hit me again, Father?"

His eyes narrowed into slits, his hand on the hilt of his sword. "I want to find out what is going on with your Birth Bind."

"What do you mean? You were there. You saw it removed. You saw it replaced. You've seen it torture me for months."

"Yes. And it's been protecting you from your curse. Did you think I haven't been making plans to shield you when you take part in the Revelation Ceremony? We're only weeks away now. Your life is in danger, and it's up to me to keep you safe. To keep you alive, ungrateful as you are."

"That's gryphon-shit. You're doing it to protect yourself," I snarled.

"You are more valuable to me than you think."

Believe it or not, Lady Lyriana is more valuable to me than just a way to hold you in check.

That's what he'd said the first night.

"I'm your son, and your heir. How am I valuable beyond that? What does that mean?"

My father clucked his tongue in disapproval, his head shaking slowly. "You've gotten very bold, Rhyan. This isn't you."

"You don't know me."

"I know this shouldn't be possible."

"Anything is possible!"

He laughed. But he was starting to sound nervous. "You're delusional if you believe that to be true. You shouldn't have been able to get a hit on me like that. And you didn't because 'anything is possible,'" he said, mocking me. "You've done something."

"I've done nothing."

"Then how?" he seethed. "How did you send your father flying across the room unless you haven't been engaging in something illegal?"

Like he never engaged in anything illegal.

His question sank in. For a second, I stopped being angry. As much as I hated to admit it, he was right about this. Even if I was the sort to fight back, even if I'd been training, I shouldn't have had access to my power. I shouldn't have been able to throw him so far.

But I'd thrown Sean. And my body had changed these past weeks, my muscles had grown. I was taller than I'd been before the summer started. And there'd been no reasonable explanation.

The door in the hall reopened again, and Bowen appeared with one of my father's spindly mages. Bowen unlocked the cell door, and the mage strolled in, his blue robes wisping behind him as he brandished his stave.

"Something's wrong with my son's Birth Bind. I need you to check it. Tell me if it's been tampered with or removed."

The mage stepped forward, lifting his stave above my head

and slowly moving it down. He repeated this gesture again and again, circling around me. Then he poked the stave at my chest, but it didn't touch me; the stave kept bumping into some sort of invisible field, like a dome of protection was encasing me. The binding. Every time the stave hit against it, gold sparks flew. He circled me, poking again and again.

"The Birth Bind is intact," the mage stated.

"No," my father argued. "This is ridiculous. He's acting too strong. There must be some hole, some leak."

"It's completely secure," the mage said. "I assure you. I've checked it twice over. It's not only secure, it's one of the strongest binds I've ever seen. Appears to be almost reinforced. The mage who performed it did a very thorough job."

"Then it's me?" I asked, staring down at my hands.

"Put your Godsdamned hands down. You're not strong. You're not special."

"Then explain the bump on the back of your head," I yelled. "Explain to me why you're afraid of me now!"

"My son is out of sorts," my father said to the mage, an icy calm in his voice that sent shivers down my spine. "He's growing bold as he nears his Revelation Ceremony. Forgetting his place beside me. Believing in possibilities that do not exist."

My heart raced. In any other circumstance like this, he would have hit me by now, knocked me senseless, had me helpless on the ground. He'd have a whip in his hand, or a blade, or a fist.

But he wasn't coming near me. He really was scared of me.

Because I had power. Because there was something inside me. Something he feared. Something he was desperate to control.

"You're afraid I can fight you," I said. "You're worried you'll lose."

"Go on then. You think that's true, fight me." He turned to the mage. "Leave us. Wait outside the cell with the soturion."

The mage did as ordered, leaving me alone behind the bars with my Arkasva.

"Well, then," my father said. "Come on. Let's have it. Show your father how strong you are."

I raced forward, my arm swinging. His fist shot out at the last second, punching the wind from my lungs. I wheezed, falling onto my back, barely able to breathe, coughing and spitting blood while gasping for air. Every part of me sore and aching.

"You see. You're not stronger than me."

I was still wheezing, but I rolled over, rose onto bruised knees and swallowed back the bile in my throat as sweat poured down my forehead. "Then how did I punch you?" I asked.

"A fluke. One that will not be repeated."

"That was no fluke. That was me! And the moment I'm unbound, I will do it again."

I expected him to charge at me, to hit me, to whip me, to draw the blade. He did nothing. And I was becoming more and more sure that I had a power I'd never known to wield. He was afraid of me. Afraid of my strength. And something else. Something I couldn't yet put my finger on.

He gestured for the mage to reenter. "My son has forgotten himself, forgotten his place in the hierarchy of Glemaria. I think he needs a reminder. Place a second bind on him."

"What? No!" I yelled, jumping to my feet. My body was already shaking, my skin burning and itching as if feeling the first bind in overflow.

"Make this one visible. Black ropes. Make sure he can see it at all times."

"Father! No! Don't!" The first one was torture enough. I couldn't stand a second.

"When you're done, you'll borrow the same magic used here by Ka Shavo. I've already paid for it. Just enough to conceal the ropes to all eyes but his," he smiled, "and to mine."

I was going to be sick. "Father, please! This is ridiculous!

I'm already bound. I can already feel it all the fucking time! I can barely sleep. I'll go mad."

"You should have thought about that before you disobeyed your Arkasva. Your Imperator. Your father."

"Please! Don't do this to me. Don't do this!"

But he was already walking away, not listening, not hearing my pleas. "Bowen, when he comes to, bring him back to his room."

"Father! Your highness! Don't! Don't!" I whimpered. "I'm bound! I can't touch you! I won't!"

I was going half-mad from the replacement Birth Bind. My skin itched as power burned beneath it, trying to break free, desperate for release after having once known freedom. And the feeling, it had been growing stronger every single day. Torturous these past weeks.

Adding another bind—one I could see all the time, one I could never forget—I'd be farther than Lethea by the time of the Revelation Ceremony. It didn't matter I only had weeks to go.

I couldn't breathe. I couldn't let him do this.

I had a window. Bowen was outside the cell. I could strike. I could take the mage. He was skinny, not a fighter, not a soturion. I'd thrown Sean. I'd punched my father—one of the greatest warriors in the Empire. I'd take down the mage next.

I rushed at him my arms swinging. And I could feel it. The power, the fire burning inside me. But the mage didn't need to be a fighter. He had a stave.

Blue sparks shot forth, and I was on my back in seconds, my entire body pulsing with pain.

The mage's sandals echoed on the floor as he stepped forward.

I opened my eyes, ready to vomit or pass out. I only had enough strength to shake my head, to whisper, "Don't."

But he did.

Black ropes coiled from the end of his stave and wrapped

around my feet. They rose like snakes up my legs, circling and tightening across my hips and stomach until they were coiled around nearly every inch of my skin.

Panic numbed me all over while my body shook, and then my world turned black.

When I woke, I was back in Cresthaven wearing a fresh black tunic, a silver gryphon emblazoned across my chest. My body felt like it had been bathed, like my skin had been scrubbed clean. Scrubbed raw. But when I stared at my arms and legs, there it was. The binding. The ropes. The reminder that I was trapped. That I was weak. Powerless. Humiliated.

I sat up. Bowen stood watch at the end of my bed.

"I'm sorry, your grace."

"You can fuck your apologies, Bowen. If you're really so Godsdamned sorry, tell me this. The truth. What is he not telling me? Why did we come here?"

"He did tell you. He wanted to bring home something valuable."

"Something? Or someone?" I snarled.

"You know the answer."

"And you couldn't warn me! You knew! You knew how I felt. Maybe you can't protect my body, but you could have at least protected *me*! Made my feelings matter! I spent the whole summer staying away from her, wasting what little time we could have had, for no fucking reason!"

"I was protecting you," he pleaded. "Because I did see. And I knew the plan. And I thought…I thought it was for the best. That it might save you some pain down the road."

"Well, it won't. Because I'm not letting it fucking happen!" I grabbed my boots, my legs aching and straining against the ropes. Even my arms felt tired and weighed down, as I pulled them over my feet, trying not to look at the binds. At the reminder of what my father had done. A plan was beginning to form. "He's in the Seating Room isn't he? Gloating."

Bowen didn't respond. It was all the confirmation I needed.

"And what are you going to do?" Bowen asked.

"Threaten him with the only leverage I have. Me."

"Your grace," he started, but I was already pushing past him to my door.

"Move aside. Now. And don't follow."

I stormed the halls, heading straight for the Seating Room, the feeling of the ropes against my skin weighing me down with each step. But that only made me more determined.

I came down the stairs into the Great Hall. Hair of fire, Batavia red, was gleaming in the center of the room's columns. The face and body of a goddess. Of Lyriana.

My heart stopped, my entire body coming to a halt. She was walking across the floor, with a stack of scrolls in her arms. Like she'd just returned from the Great Library. She looked like she was carrying a month's worth of reading.

"Rhyan," she said, stopping when she saw me. Her voice bright, hopeful. Sweet. Gods, I loved hearing her say my name.

I stepped down from the last step, my boots hitting the marble floor as rainbow lights from the windows shined over us.

My heart was pounding, ready to burst from my chest. Fuck, I wanted her. To kiss her. To hold her. To ask what scrolls she had, and if I could read beside her again. What I wouldn't give to spend the afternoon in her library on the couch, just watching her read. And then after awhile, sliding my hand behind her neck, tangling my fingers in her soft hair, drawing those perfect lips to mine, and kissing her until we were dizzy, until I was sliding over her body, the scrolls discarded, rolling across the floor.

She started forward, an almost puzzled expression on her face as I realized I hadn't responded.

Because it was already over, before it had barely begun.

"Your grace," I said politely, my stomach twisting. It didn't matter how much I wanted her, needed her, desired her with all my being, it was over. I had to end it. Now.

She took one more step, and the entire stack of scrolls exploded from her arms, falling to the ground and rolling in every direction across the marble beneath us.

I rushed forward, crouching low before her, gathering each scroll I could reach, noting the High Lumerian on each label. A small, sad smile spread across my lips. I knew she wanted more, wanted to be something other than the third daughter, the youngest sister, the one relegated to the sidelines. Her aunt Arianna was now Master of Education on the Bamarian Council.

But Lyr really did love reading and studying, and I loved that about her.

I froze. Loved that about her, or...? I could still barely process that truth. Barely handle it. Barely accept it with what I was about to do.

I swallowed hard, my eyes meeting hers. Her cheeks were flushed, nearly the same color as those lips. Those soft lips I could still feel against mine, still taste. And for a second, all my resolve was gone. I was back there; it was just me and her under the tree, lost in each other's arms, our lips tangled, our bodies seeking each other's. The kiss had nearly consumed me last night, and I knew now, the memory of it would never let me go.

I began handing the scrolls back to her, carefully placing them in her arms, both of us still crouched together. I caught sight of my arm, the black rope coiled across it. I pulled back, worried she'd see, waiting for her to comment.

But she didn't notice. They were invisible to her. Instead, she looked up, and gave me a shy, vulnerable smile. "How are you?"

I shrugged, balancing on my heels. "I didn't sleep well. You?"

"Um, fine. I didn't see you back at the party. Was every-thing...um.... Last night..." She bit her lip.

"Lyr," I said, feeling sick. Feeling ready to vomit. "You should know that I'm probably leaving soon with my father."

She blinked. "Already? But...I thought you were here

another few weeks. Your father even put an order in for a second litter to be custom made for the journey home."

A second litter. For her. Shit. No. No.

And I knew with even greater clarity, knew exactly what I had to do. Knew the secrets Bowen had tried to keep from me. Knew what my father had unwittingly admitted. Even if I didn't understand it all. It was enough. Enough for me to do what I had to do to save her.

Lyr was going to remain in Bamaria. She was not going to marry Kane. She was going to marry who she wished, and by the Gods, live a life that made her happy. That gave her more than the path she saw laid out before her.

She set the scrolls aside on the ground and reached out, touching my arm. I stiffened, and stared down in shame, seeing the ropes covering my body. They stretched across my tunic around the silver gryphon emblazoned on the front.

Can you imagine a rope holding this one down?

That was all I was. A gryphon tied down by some rope. And the rope had won.

But the difference was gryphons were tied with regular rope; I was trapped in a magic binding. He'd had to cheat to beat me.

"He's going to cancel the order," I said. "We have urgent business back at home."

"Business that requires an heir? What if you stayed?" she asked. "You still have time before your Revelation Ceremony to extend the visit. There's so much of Bamaria you haven't seen yet. I could show you. Maybe even tour one of the other pyramids in the Great Library."

"I'm sure that'd be lovely. But I'm ready to return home, too," I said, my voice cold. "I'm planning to leave by nightfall."

Her face fell as she slid her hand off my arm. I was breaking her heart. Fuck. I was a monster. A mess. A Godsdamned gryphon-shit asshole.

But I wasn't free to be with her. And she wasn't free, either —even if she didn't know it yet. This was for the best.

"But, last night you…"

"Your grace, I…." I reached for her arm, one final touch. My jaw tensed. It was all I could do not to slide my hand across her arm, to her neck, to cup her cheek, to touch her hair, to pull her close. I pulled back. Then I restacked the scrolls, and placed them in her arms. "Got them?" I stood up, moving away from her.

She nodded, something broken in her expression. She rose to her feet. "Yes. Thank you."

"Enjoy your scrolls."

"Thanks," she said, her voice shaking.

I probably wouldn't see her again. I was going to propose to my father we get the hell out of Bamaria the minute I made my demands. If we stayed, he'd get ideas again, and I couldn't risk that.

If we stayed, I might lose my will. I might seek her out. I might confess everything.

I walked away from her, refusing to turn back, not even for one last look. I was terrified I'd say screw it, push her against the wall, let the scrolls fly, and kiss her until I was dizzy. Kiss her until she was moaning again, until her breasts were pressed against me, and I was wild with want and desire, and need.

I screwed my eyes shut. My hands were shaking. No more.

I found my father exactly where I expected him to be. He stood before Arkasva Batavia in the Seating Room.

"I need to speak to you. Alone. Now," I said.

Arkasva Batavia looked stunned at my outburst, but offered a small chuckle. "I'll leave you two."

"There's no need, your grace," my father snarled. "Rhyan, now is not the time."

But Arkasva Batavia only smiled indulgently at me. "It's fine. I need a break from these negotiations anyway. And don't worry overmuch for the interruption. I have three daughters. Four actually. I understand. Better to handle this now, I'm sure. How about we reconvene in an hour?"

"Yes," my father said, his hand on the hilt of his sword, his expression murderous. The moment the door closed, and we were alone, he snarled, "You thought this would end well for you?"

"We're leaving," I announced. "Right now. Cancel this meeting. Pack your things. Order your men. Have the litter prepared. *Your highness.*"

"Did you hit your head this morning?"

"I'm thinking more clearly than I ever have."

"Then go back to your room before I use this on you." His fingers brushed the hilt, the black leather gleaming.

"You can cut me. I don't care. But I'm not leaving until you agree to my terms. We pack up. We leave today, just us. And whatever contract you have in place for Kane, whatever negotiation you're doing right now, you undo it. You tear it up."

"This morning's lesson wasn't enough for you?" He wrapped his fingers around the hilt, the sound of steel sliding as he lifted the blade, only enough to reveal a slither of its shine. "Want to see some cuts beneath those ropes?"

"Go ahead," I said. "You can beat me. You can cut me. You're still going to listen and do what I say. Lyriana isn't coming to Glemaria. She's not marrying Arkturion Kane. Whatever scheme led you here, you have failed. It's over, and we are going home with nothing."

"I thought the binding would knock some sense into you. I can have those ropes tightened. I can have them heated as well, or frozen. And by the Gods, Rhyan, I think I will. But your actions now will determine how hot. How cold."

"You will meet my demands," I said. I wasn't playing his mind games anymore. "You will do so because you showed your hand today. You're afraid of me. You know I'm stronger than you."

"Stronger? I knocked you out."

"And before that, I knocked you across the cell! You're supposed to be the greatest fucking warrior in Glemaria—in the north. And I'm bound, so explain that."

"One punch does not a warrior make." His nostrils flared.

"You needed to put two binds on me to contain me, my power, my strength."

"That's meaningless. The mage was wrong. The rebinding spell was faulty. And I showed nothing. You do not order your Arkasva, your Imperator. What you're playing with now—this is treason. You know what the punishment is for treason?"

"Death," I said, calmly.

"Exactly."

I walked toward him, my arms and legs heavy from the bindings, my stomach twisting. Like a viper, I struck, grabbing the hilt of his sword from his hand. I withdrew it all the way out, brandishing it before him, watching the gleam of the steel beneath the crackling torches of the Seating Room. "Looks like you need me to sharpen it again." I tossed the blade into my palm, the hilt pointing toward my father, the tip aimed at my belly. "Go on then. Take it. Kill me."

The sword was in his hands in seconds. And then back in its sheath. It was his fist that came for me, that cracked against my jaw.

I stumbled back, but I straightened. He wasn't going to kill me. Because I was valuable to him. Like Lyriana was valuable to him. And he wasn't going to control either of us.

"Here's what's going to happen," I said, coughing back blood. "You let go of your design on Lyriana, and we go home. And I remain your obedient son. If you do not do this, I will march straight to Imperator Kormac's quarters, or make an appearance at the home of Lord Tristan Grey. Either one will do.

And I will tell them exactly what you did on my birthday. Ka Grey hunt vorakh—did you know that? And I've made quite an enemy with Tristan—he'd be only too happy to take me in, report me to the Emperor. And Imperator Kormac? Do you think for a second he would not love to gain the upper hand against the only other man in the Empire who can claim to be his equal in power? Do you think your little alliance would survive the chance for him to beat you?"

"Now I know you're farther than Lethea. You do that, you tell anyone you have a vorakh, and you're dead. They'll kill you."

"Do you think I care? Because I know what happened to Ka Azria. If they kill me, they'll kill you, too. Imperator Kormac and the Emperor would love that. But I don't think you would."

"They wouldn't just kill me," he said, his voice low. "You would condemn your mother to death. Threaten her. Keeping your vorakh secret also protects her. Are you that much of a monster?"

I shrugged. "And you're not? You threaten her daily. Maybe death would be kinder. Maybe at least death would save her from you."

"Give me your arm, you're swearing a blood oath right fucking now."

I shook my head. "Funny thing about blood oaths—you can break them. Go ahead." I held out my arm. "Put one on me. It ends the same. I'll tell. Either today, or tomorrow, or in a month. Whenever I can. And I'll be dead. And the Emperor's soturi will be at your steps."

My father was turning red. I'd never seen him like this before, so angry, so stunned. He'd never looked more dangerous. More cornered.

But I knew at last—I had him. I'd won.

"You will pay for this. I will not forget. A day will come, when the debt is paid. When the punishment for this crime is too great for you to bear. And I will remind you of this. Of the day you asked for pain. For punishment. Do not fool yourself into believing you are strong. You are weak. You must resort to petty, childish threats. To keep my ungrateful, idiotic excuse for a son and heir alive, I will agree. The contract is null. But you are not stronger than me. Do you hear me?"

"I hear you," I said. "And I promise you, that a day will come when my power is unleashed and my binds are broken."

"You've made a huge mistake. That girl has the potential to unleash more power and destruction than anyone in the Empire ever has. You will rue the day we did not control it."

My heart pounded, my mouth dry.

He was lying. He had to be. How could he know that? She was three years from her Revelation Ceremony. She was third in line.

But Afeya were after her, too....

"You're playing in an arena where you don't know the rules. Where this victory is only one small battle. You have not won the war. You will never be strong enough."

"Not today," I said, and turned around. My back to my father. "Give me time."

~

T held my breath until I reached my room, walking stiffly until I was outside on the balcony, my hands gripping the railing.

And then, only then, did I sob. It all caught up to me—the stress, the weight of what I'd carried all summer, the relief of knowing I'd succeeded, and the grief—the grief of what I was giving up.

My heart was breaking and coming to life all at once. I knew I was in love with Lyriana Batavia—that I loved her with my whole soul and my heart. And I needed to forget her.

"Your grace," Bowen called, his voice unsure. I knew he'd heard me. Knew he'd heard my cries. And I didn't have it in me to care.

But I wiped at my eyes, swallowed and tried to compose myself as I turned to see Jules heading through the door and stepping out onto the balcony.

"You gryphon-shit asshole!" She raised her hand, her face fierce and angry like that of a lioness, as she raced towards me. "She's crying because of you! What the fuck, Rhyan!"

But then her expression softened, her hand fell, her eyes seeing the cut on my jaw, already swelling.

"She is?" I asked, my heart breaking. I blinked back my own fresh tears before they could fall, and bit the inside of my cheek. "Go ahead, Jules. I'm sure I deserve whatever slap you had planned. But if it makes you feel better, I already had the shit beat out of me this morning. And last night."

Her eyes searched mine then ran down my arms and legs. She couldn't see the ropes, but she was perceptive. She knew something was wrong. Her eyes searched mine, with more concern than I was ready for. "What did they do to you?"

I waved it off. "It's fine. It was a price worth paying." I exhaled sharply. "She's safe now. It's done."

"What?" Jules asked. "Rhyan, what is going on? What did you do?"

"What I had to."

"And that included breaking her heart?"

"I think…." I swallowed. "I think I broke mine, too." I laughed, the sound cheerless. "It was worth it. She's safe."

"Auriel's bane. I was so ready to slap you. That was her first kiss, asshole. And you really…." She groaned. "I can't even be mad at you right now. You really do look like your heart's breaking."

Like being given the love of your life only for your heart to shrivel up the day you met her.

Those had been my own stupid thoughts about a deal with Afeya on the journey here. I hadn't even made one. Hadn't even spoken to one. Not technically. I'd simply seen one. Two. And I still had that fate. A dance, a kiss, my heart opening and coming to life, only to break the next day. Which reminded me, I needed to warn her.

"Jules, there's been Afeya stalking around Bamaria. Watching Lyr, talking about her. That's why I danced with her last night. I didn't mean…" I bit my lip. "I didn't mean for the other things to happen between us. I didn't mean to hurt her. But they were approaching. So, I intervened."

Jules gasped. "What?" She hugged her arms across her chest, goosebump rising on her skin. "Afeya…" Her hands moved up and down her arms as she processed my words. "Thank you. Rhyan, thank you for doing that. I…I haven't seen anything. Haven't ever seen them around. But…I'm going to let her guard know."

"Good." I gripped the banister, staring at the waves crash against the shore. It really was beautiful. And peaceful. "Jules? You've never heard anything about Lyr being extra powerful before, have you? Or heard talk that there's something special about her, something magical I mean?"

Jules shrugged, shifting beside me. "Just in the way that all of the bloodline of Ka Batavia are. I mean, politically…sure. But, no. Nothing magical. Why?"

"I don't know. Just speculation." I turned back to Jules. "Keep an extra eye on her for me."

"I always do."

"Thank you," I said.

We stood in silence for several minutes before she finally asked, "So, you're leaving?"

"Tonight."

She smiled sadly. "Despite your desperate need of further

lessons in how to have fun, I think I'm going to miss you. Not as much as she will, but…"

"You've been a good friend, Jules. I might even miss you a little."

"Thanks for the overwhelming show of emotion. You've been a good friend, too. More than you know. Good luck with your Revelation Ceremony."

I laughed. "Thanks. I'll need it. And same with yours next year."

"Why don't you wish me good luck a little closer to the event?"

I shook my head. "I don't think our paths will cross again."

"You never know." She winked. "Anything is possible."

I exhaled again, my breath shaky. That would mean me coming here. Seeing Lyr. I couldn't imagine any circumstances that would allow for it. But I hoped she was right.

"Hey, Rhyan? You know how I'm incredibly perceptive, good at spotting liars, keeping secrets, and being adorable, as well as the living, breathing darling of Bamaria?"

"Your list of attributes are endless," I said flatly.

"I'm also a hopeless romantic. And I'm rooting for you two."

I swallowed, my eyes burning, as I wrapped her into a tight hug, grateful she hugged me back. Grateful we could have this one pure moment, not shadowed by Imperator Kormac.

"Gods," she groaned, as she pulled back. "You're going to make it very hard for me to pretend I hate you while Lyr gets over you."

"Hate me," I said. "Do whatever to help her. Make her feel better. And keep her safe."

"I promise. Take care of yourself, your grace."

"You, too, my lady."

She smiled again. "Okay, asshole. See you later."

～

At nightfall, I watched the outline of Cresthaven, a dark silhouette against the starry night sky, fade into the distance for the brief moment my father left the curtains open. Blue lights glowed as the ashvan raced by. And then I was trapped again, back in the litter for weeks alone with him, now with ropes around my entire body.

But I'd realized something. Yes, my father was a brute. A cruel monster. And he was still stronger than me in every way that mattered. I was still a prisoner under his control. But I'd fought back. I'd found strength I never believed I'd have.

I'd found a chink in his armor. Lyr had helped me do that, even if she'd never know.

He absorbed himself in a scroll, so angry with me for once, he couldn't speak to or look at me. I'd pay a higher price at home. I knew that much. But it was worth it. I had no regrets.

I stared at my hand. A small cut down my palm. I'd done it myself. Not a blood oath. But a personal promise. I'd found a way to save Lyr, at least save her from my father. I was going to do the same for my mother. I was going to get her out of Glemaria. Get her away from my father.

Or die trying.

I reached into my belt pouch, realizing I needed to apply a fresh batch of sunleaves to the wound. But instead of the cured paste, I pulled out a single golden leaf. After I'd finished packing, after I'd sworn to save my mother, I'd returned to the field and found the exact suntree where it had happened. Where we had kissed, where my heart had been forged. Where my soul had come alive.

I clutched the leaf, looking at the contrast of pure gold as it shined against the black ropes across my pale arms, against the red cut of my promise.

I swore to myself, right then and there, a day would come when I was even stronger, when I would fight back. And on that day, I would win. I would tear this rope apart. Tear it to fucking pieces.

And then, who knew? Maybe my destiny with Lyriana hadn't been written in stone. Maybe Uncle Sean and Jules had been right. Anything was possible.

Maybe our journey wasn't over, maybe this was simply a seed, still growing, on its way to becoming a suntree.

LADY OF THE DROWNED EMPIRE

THE STORY CONTINUES IN THE DROWNED EMPIRE SERIES, #3

Lady of the Drowned Empire

SON OF THE DROWNED EMPIRE

RHYAN'S STORY CONTINUES IN THE DROWNED
EMPIRE SERIES 1.5

Son of the Drowned Empire

SON OF THE DROWNED EMPIRE: CHAPTER ONE

(One year after solstice)

"Shhh," I whispered. "I've got you now. I've—*fuck*!"

The baby gryphon squawking like a maniac in my arms had been absolutely feral since I found him and had just attempted to bite a chunk out of my hand.

"Godsdamnit," I growled. "I'm trying to help you."

As a show of gratitude for saving his life, the little beast bit me again, this time drawing blood. Drops fell to my bedroom floor before I could stop them, and I shook my head. I was always cleaning up blood.

The gryphon's eyes snapped up to mine, pale silver and full of innocence and confusion. I sighed in defeat. His heart was beating too quickly against my palm, his tiny body shaking. He was scared. Hurt. Definitely hungry.

My own stomach grumbled.

I could relate.

Yelling at him obviously wasn't helping. So, I cradled the little beast against my chest, smoothing the back of his head, and gently squeezing his neck where his baby furs shifted to feathers. "It's all right now," I soothed. My aura flared out, covering him in the cold his species preferred, winter cold, Glemarian cold, the cold that clung to my body at all times since my aura had been released.

His eyes closed, and with the tiniest pathetic squawk, he at last snuggled against me—at least, he snuggled as much as a gryphon could. I pulled him closer. "That's a good boy," I gritted through my teeth, the wounds on my palms smarting.

Shifting him so his baby legs were exposed, I was able to see his left back leg hadn't been merely twisted like I'd thought, but broken, explaining the ruckus outside my window. I'd spotted him immediately and without thinking made my way down the mountain's side, not expecting to fight for my life as I tried to save his.

Had he been right under my window, the rescue would have been simple—a quick opening of the glass panes and one grab, and it'd have been over. But he'd been quite a way below, stuck on a jut of Gryphon's Mount, lying helplessly with nowhere to go. Too young to fly, he should have had only three options: one, to fall to his death; two, to be scooped up by another gryphon, if one was willing to touch him; or, three, to starve until death claimed him.

The secret I carried, the ability I'd been forced to hide for over a year and a half, had made me his unlikely fourth option. I was vorakh, cursed with forbidden magic—traveling—the third and most feared of the three powers banned by the Lumerian Empire. This magic had allowed me to vanish from my bedroom and land on the side of the mountain beneath my Ka's fortress. The toes of my boots had desperately clung to the rock as I wrestled the terrified gryphon into my arms while my soturion cloak flapped wildly in the breeze.

I slipped and nearly fell to my death three times before I'd wrangled him out of his nook and reappeared with us both in my bedroom, my chest heaving from exertion. Bells had pounded into the cold morning sky, announcing the hour. It was the tail-end of summer, and we were still experiencing our warmest days of the year, but being this far north meant our mornings remained chilly—though not chilly enough to keep me from getting drenched during my rescue mission. My sweat had already turned cold against my forehead and neck.

Now, my own heart was hammering as the reality of what I'd done sank in. I'd broken *his* rules. I risked everything I'd sworn to protect—everything I fought for, suffered for—without even a second thought. All for one crying gryphon.

I squeezed my eyes shut, my stomach churning. *Fuck.* I'd been so good; I hadn't traveled for an entire month. It'd felt as if, after a year of forcing my will and tempering down my emotions, I'd finally gotten the power under control, and found the strength to suppress it. Gaining dominance over it, over my emotions, had been necessary, not just to avoid his wrath, but because he knew when I slipped. He always knew. And he always punished accordingly because if anyone else ever discovered the truth—if anyone else saw me vanish or suddenly appear —our lives were forfeit. Not just mine and his, but my mother's also. One slip, one mistake, and there'd be a one-way trip to Lethea for my Ka.

And one did not come back from Lethea.

I bit the inner corner of my cheek, as I perked up my ears for any shouts of my father's guards coming to drag me before him. Bowen, my personal escort and bodyguard, sometimes yelled my name to wake me, even on mornings I was permitted to sleep in. This had been one of those mornings. The Glemarian Academy was not yet in session. We were a week past Auriel's Feast Day. Tonight, we would celebrate the Oath Ceremony, the forming of *kashonim* between apprentices and the newly made novice mages and soturi.

Technically, I'd been on break from classes for the past week. I was still required to train for the purposes of maintaining my strength and stamina, but I was free to appear in the

Katurium whenever I felt like it. I could train as long as I pleased. I would lose this freedom in two days' time when the Academy's classes resumed, and I returned to my apprentice's brutal training regimen.

If Bowen had any idea that I'd spent part of my morning dangling from the side of the mountain after having used forbidden magic to get to it, I was fucked. He'd never admit it out loud, as he'd never be allowed to speak such things even if he wanted to, but Bowen knew my secret, too. No one could spend as many hours as he did guarding me and not know the truth about my vorakh. I had no doubt he'd reported me to my father each time he witnessed my body fade in and out of existence, confirming what my Imperator and my Arkasva already seemed to know.

The bells came to a crashing halt, a cool breeze singing in their absence. The wind carried the deep squawking growls of the fully grown gryphons soaring overhead.

The one in my arms whimpered as the clouds passed and the bright golden sun streamed through my window. And only then, safely removed from the shadows of the cliff and the danger of falling to our deaths, did I get a real look at what I'd risked my life for. There'd been a reason I'd seen him so easily from afar, a reason I'd launched into action, and a reason he'd been in danger.

My throat tightened. This was no Glemarian gryphon I held. His feathers were not made of the muted grays and browns of the creatures that filled our skies. They were not even the bronze or silver of the prized gryphons we'd bred and raised for centuries. This little one had feathers and fur made of the brightest, most fiery red.

Batavia red.

The thought came so suddenly I almost stumbled forward.

My stomach twisted, the backs of my eyes on fire, before I brushed all memories of *her* away. Her name in the back of my thoughts felt like a dream I could barely grasp, one I struggled to recall. And yet... she was a dream whose images had been burned into my mind. Branded onto my body. Imprinted onto my heart.

My soul.

Hazel eyes flecked with gold stared up at me beneath the golden leaves of the sun tree. The scent of vanilla musk in the air wrapped around my body, and the warm breeze of a summer night blew through my hair as her soft fingers tangled in my curls at the nape of my neck. Her gasp was a kiss against my lips, leaving shivers all over my body. My blood pumping...

I blinked back the image and shook off the sensation.

She was safe. That was all that mattered. She was safe because of me; I'd bargained with the only thing I had left in the fight—my secret. My shame. My silence. All I had possessed had been given freely in exchange for her freedom.

One year ago, I'd sworn to my father that if he touched her, if he set his sights on her again, I'd reveal our secret. I'd damn the whole Ka, my family, and even my mother. It had been the first battle against him I ever won, but the victory had cost me.

And just like that, there was a flash of black ropes tied around my hands and arms. Too tight, too hot. My skin burned and itched; my breath came short.

No. No.

I blinked, and the ropes vanished. My arms were clear, my hands unbound.

I took a deep breath. I was alone in my room holding the gryphon. No ropes bound my body. There was nothing tied around me. There never would be again. As long as I stayed under his radar, as long as I kept our secret, I was safe. *She* was safe.

That was more than I could say for the little one in my arms, twitching in his sleep.

The red feathers and fur were not natural to Glemaria, nor any part of the Lumerian Empire.

I'd rescued an Afeyan gryphon.

I had been horrified when I'd realized a baby was trapped down there, but I hadn't stopped to think, to question *why*? Now I knew. It was his Afeyan coloring that damned him.

Gryphons were sacred in Glemaria. For centuries, they'd appeared on the sigil of Ka Hart: silver gryphon wings beneath a golden sun. We'd even named the Godsdamned mountain we were on after them. The beasts filled our skies, patrolled hourly for akadim, and transported us back and forth across the north. Severe fines were given to anyone found guilty of harm or cruelty to the animals. Worse punishments had been written into law for the purposeful or accidental killing of gryphons, but only if they were of the Lumerian breeds.

When Afeyan gryphons from the Night Lands crossed into our territory, they were to be shot down on sight. I'd only heard of it happening a dozen times in my life, though in the last year alone, that number had tripled. It was as if the Night Lands were testing our defenses, trying to see how hard they could push, how many of their brightly colored gryphons they could send through our skies before we'd retaliate or figure out what the hell their purpose was. Afeya were always up to something, and it was never good. I knew that well.

And here I was, harboring the enemy, saving his life.

Rescuing a hurt baby gryphon should have made me a hero in my father's court. Were I to be caught with this one, though... I looked down at him, his red feathers soft, his eyes so big, shiny, trusting. He was just a baby. I couldn't abandon him.

Whatever game the Afeya or Queen Ishtara were playing at, this creature was innocent.

I sucked on my bleeding finger and wrapped the gryphon more tightly in my cloak, hiding his body, drawing on my aura to keep him cold and quiet. Then, I headed toward my door. I still hadn't heard a word from behind it nor received any summons from my father. Possibly, I was in the clear. But still, my heart pounded and my body tensed. I was risking a lot. And for what?

I unbolted the lock and opened my bedroom door.

"Morning, your grace." Bowen was leaning against the wall opposite my room, his eyes half-open, not even looking at me.

I strode forward and slapped his shoulder with my free hand. "My enemies are truly trembling at my defenses."

He opened one eye all the way, a retort on the edge of his lips, before he shrugged, pushing his leathers back into place over his shoulder.

Bowen was more of a statement than a true protector when I was home. No enemy would dare attack me here—except for one, the one whom Bowen dared not stop. And because of that, he was often sleeping on the job, or not even paying attention at all. Except when he could get me in trouble.

"Katurium?" he asked, eyeing my armor.

I locked my elbow against my side, my green cloak concealing the gryphon. "No. I'm off to Artem's," I announced, knowing Bowen hated the stench of the stables more than anything. Hopefully, that would keep him from following too closely.

He cursed under his breath as I'd expected, and only as I rounded the hall did I hear his footsteps pick up, echoing on the gray stone floor behind me.

The gryphon squeaked, suddenly alert, and I coughed loudly to cover up the sound before craning my head forward and cooing, "*Shhh, tovayah, tovayah.*"

He calmed and quieted, but if he made another sound, I was fucked. I picked up my speed, my pulse racing, both out of nerves at the thought of being caught and at the effort it took to not let my emotions take me away. I had to walk calmly but quickly; I could not allow my magic to interfere and transport me to my destination.

I'd become rather good at stopping my magic, but I could always slip without warning.

A few minutes later, I'd made my way outside, a practiced scowl on my face as I passed a line of my father's personal soturi. Their blank eyes seemed to glaze over me, I'd learned long ago not to drop my guard before them. They were obsessively, annoyingly aware of every move made by the Heir Apparent to the Arkasva and Imperator to the North. My father would have their heads if they fucked up.

Luckily, my habit of spending early mornings in the stables was well known, and it had been a long time since they'd really paid attention to my current route. Still, I held my breath, eyeing them as I passed, my scowl deepening. Hand-picked by my father, every soturion standing before me was a right-shit asshole. Right-shit assholes forced to bow as I passed.

I pulled open the gates and was immediately blasted with the pungent scents of fresh gryphon-shit and hay. My little gryphon squawked to life, wings fluttering inside my cloak.

"Shhh!" I hissed. "Not yet."

I stepped forward into the stables, built like a giant arena. This was the training ground for gryphons, the place where they learned to transport us, to hunt what we sought, to follow our orders, and to remember their place.

Each stable was built with open walls that reached toward the domed ceiling; seven stories high. I greeted several of the stable hands, carefully making my way toward the stalls closest to Artem's office. He was occupied, dealing with a fully grown gryphon who'd been rather moody the past few weeks.

Before I could announce myself, Artem turned, having sensed me. He'd been doing that since I was a boy. "Good morning, Lord Rhyan, your grace."

His gruff voice rose above the chaos of the gryphon calls. He stepped back from his stall and slapped his thigh—his version of a bow since he had a bad back—then returned to his post. His gaze focused on the gryphon before him. "Down!" he yelled. "*Dorscha!*" The beast sat back on its giant haunches; its beak turned in submission. It received a nod from Artem, who tossed a steak into the air.

The gryphon's wings spread, its talons lifting from the ground as it flew up to catch its breakfast. With a surge of energy, its bronzed wings flapped, creating a gust of wind that pushed the hay across its stall out toward Artem. I'd seen this happen so many times, I was positive the scent of hay sticks and gryphon-shit had been permanently etched into Artem's body.

The gryphon growled as it came to a halt from a tug on its leg by the rope that kept it grounded. The baby squeaked in response, shaking and suddenly very awake and once more feral in my arms.

"Lord Rhyan." There was a warning note in Artem's voice as his eyes pierced me. Two fuzzy eyebrows turned down as he observed the rapid movements behind my cloak and the look of guilt across my face. "The fuck did you do now?"

I gave him a rather purposeful cough, my eyebrows narrowed. To be fair, I had already broken two laws this morning, and I hadn't even had my coffee yet. But since I was the Heir Apparent, it wasn't Artem's job to question me.

"Your grace," he added through gritted teeth, nostrils flaring as his eyes darted back to the movement beneath my cloak.

"Please just..." I felt suddenly desperate. What if he refused me?

"Please what, your grace?" He rubbed some loose straws of hay that had stuck to his hands onto his pants.

"I didn't realize when I first found him, Artem. He's hurt." I moved toward the only closed space in the stables, Artem's office, jerking my chin for him to follow. He frowned but pulled a thick loop of keys from his belt and unlocked the door, ushering me inside.

With the door locked behind me, I opened my cloak to reveal

the fiery red feathers of the gryphon, who was wide awake now and squawking angrily. One glance up at me though, his silver eyes watching me closely, and the gryphon softened.

Artem's eyes widened, first seeing the broken leg and then its coloring. "Auriel's bane, I..." He blew air through his lips, looking almost sick. "Where?"

"Right on my windowsill," I lied. "Leg's broken."

"I can see that." Artem was already reaching a hand out for the baby's leg, making a hushing sound as he grazed over the break. "Nasty fall. Assuming he hitched a ride with the mother who was shot down." He scooped the baby into his arms, his shoulders heaving with a tired sigh. The gryphon screeched in panic, a red wing reaching back for me. "I'll make it quick. Painless for the lad."

"No!" I pulled the gryphon back to my chest. His wings fluttered rapidly against me, as he buried his head in my leathered armor. "Artem, the fuck! He's a baby."

"It's Afeyan."

"So? I came here for you to fix his leg."

Artem rolled his eyes. "Did you now? So, it could die with its leg in a cast?"

"So, you could help him," I snarled. The gryphon's agitation was growing. He seemed to be attempting to dig his way through my armor to crawl inside. I rubbed the back of his head, shifting my hold on his trembling body. One small talon wrapped around my finger.

"Oh, aye? And what then? I cast its leg, and it dies anyway once it's seen, and then I'm, what? Thrown into prison? Awaiting pardon from the Heir Apparent? You know your father's law. Afeyan gryphons are shot down on sight."

"Grown gryphons," I countered. That was exactly how the law had been stated. Nowhere did it say we were obligated to kill the Afeyan babies who entered Glemaria. It was a loophole I planned to exploit for all its worth.

Artem bit his lip, almost looking swayed. Then, he set his jaw. "Forget it. I'm not keeping this one alive and hidden just to kill it later when it's grown. We've enough to take care of here."

I was starting to feel hysterical. He was a fucking baby! He wasn't responsible for any of his homeland's crimes. He wasn't able to understand what was happening to him, too young to process his own pain. He was alone and injured, and no one else would protect him, something he seemed to realize with how tightly he was holding onto me.

We'd come a long way in our relationship since he'd bitten me.

"Lord Rhyan, your grace, I don't mean to insult you, but you're too soft on helpless things," Artem growled, grabbing the gryphon from me again. "It's going to get you into trouble."

"Artem," I said, my voice full of the command of an Heir Apparent, of the Heir to the Imperator, the cold future ruler of Glemaria, which Artem Godsdamned well knew.

"Speak like that to me all you want, your grace. You think I forgot you outranked me before your balls dropped? It means gryphon-shit here." Artem rolled his eyes but rummaged through the drawers of his desk before pulling out a small broken gryphon harness. He unwound the worn leather from the buckle and slammed it on the table, shaking his head. "We both know what will happen if your father knows what we're up to."

I slowly processed his words and the appearance of the harness. "What *we're* up to?" I barely dared to breathe. "You'll help?"

Artem's face was scrunched in annoyance. "Aye. You're right about the law. You can't shoot a baby gryphon from the skies because a baby gryphon can't fly. But I'm not staking my life on some legal loophole. You hear me? It can stay until its leg is healed, until it can take its first flight. Not a minute longer. When that moment comes, you're going to set it free. If it makes its way back to those accursed Afeyan lands, so be it. If it's shot down, don't say I didn't warn you. And then we *never* speak of this again. Not if you want to come back here."

I nodded, the small knot in my stomach loosening. "Thank you, Artem. Truly."

"Oh, fuck off."

"I could have you punished for speaking to me like that," I said, trying to lighten the mood. I even narrowed my eyebrows in disapproval.

Artem smirked. "Believe me, Lord Rhyan, your presence is punishment enough." He rolled his eyes again, reaching for a glass vial on his work table. The gryphon was beginning to cry, a shaky, squeaking growl, his voice full of pain.

I moved to the other side of the table, holding the gryphon's head, his feathery fur soft in my hands, as I made shushing sounds. Artem tapped a few drops into his mouth. Instantly, his silver eyes widened. He looked ready to riot over whatever Artem had fed him, but then he fell silent, falling gently back asleep before offering one final trusting glance up at me. I smiled grimly before I pulled my hands away.

"Make yourself useful, at least," Artem said. "I have chores I can't get to now, thanks to some meddling pompous heir."

It was an empty request. I was here almost every morning before soturion training, helping Artem with his chores. Had been for years. When I was a boy, Lord Draken, my father's Second and Glemaria's Master of the Horse, had brought me to the stables with him for training. And then Artem took me under his wing as Lord Draken's duties pulled him away. It was one of the only places I could go where I could breathe, even with the stench of gryphon-shit surrounding me. I liked being around the beasts. I liked feeling as if I did some good in this Gods-forsaken world, something more than just being the Heir Apparent, something more than just being trained to become my father.

Before I could leave the office, there was a violent pounding on the door and a strangled yelp from outside. A fight was breaking out.

On instinct, I reached for my dagger.

"Stand down," Bowen yelled, his command carrying clearly through the door.

Artem was already moving: throwing the harness back in the drawer, covering the gryphon with a cloth, and stashing him behind the desk. The knock pounded again.

"Myself to fucking Moriel, your grace." Artem's already pale face turned white. "Were you seen?"

"I didn't think so." My fingers tightened around the hilt.

The shouts and stomps of more soturi echoed outside the office door.

"Open in the name of the Imperator." The yell came from another soturion, one I thought came from my father's escort, one of the assholes who'd watched me outside.

"Auriel's fucking balls," Artem growled as he unlocked and opened the door.

"I'm his grace's escort. I'll take him." Bowen, along with three soturi from my father's escort, crowded into Artem's office, where, despite Bowen's words, my father's soturi sprang into action.

One soturion turned his ire on Bowen, restraining him from moving forward and dragging him back out of Artem's office. The other two lurched toward me, grabbing my arms and forcing them behind my back, their fingers digging into my wrists.

I growled under my breath. Though these were the Soturi of Ka Hart, and all had sworn their lives, loyalty, and swords to my father, they were all the blood of Ka Gaddayan, the Ka of Arkturion Kane. And he was a monster.

"Soturion Baynan, what is the meaning of this? Answer me," I demanded.

Artem retreated to a back corner of his office, his eyebrows narrowing as he realized none of the soturi appeared to have come for him.

"Your father sent for you, Your Grace," snapped Baynan. He was a first cousin of Arkturion Kane, a fact that had made him far too bold for his own good. At some point, Ka Gaddayan had taken it upon themselves to take their posts a little more seriously than they ever had before. They were harsher with their judgments, quicker with their hits, and all seemed to worship the floor Kane stood upon. The more they worshipped him, the less respect they showed for me.

Bowen twisted in his restraint outside the door, his neck turning red. "Which is why I said I'd bring him," he shouted as he freed himself from the soturion holding him captive, another lesser noble related to Kane who fell face forward, his nose an inch from a fresh pile of gryphon-shit. Bowen rushed back into the office, reaching for his dagger. "I'm sworn to go by his side."

"Yes, but His Highness didn't tell you to bring him." Baynan tightened his grip on me, the shadow of a smile on his lips. He was loving this—overpowering me, overpowering my escort. "He told *me* to. Your oath holds no weight."

Bowen looked ready to riot. "My oath is everything!"

I flexed my fingers behind my back, grounding into my heels. Since my Birth Bind had been fully lifted, I'd grown stronger than anyone truly knew, than every soturion in my year, than half the anointed soturi picked exclusively for my father's guard. I could fight Baynan off me without breaking a sweat, and the asshole on my other side as well. I was powerful enough, but I wasn't fast enough to fight the next half dozen soturi armed and lined up outside the door—not without my vorakh.

My eyes narrowed on Baynan's hateful face. "He told you what?"

"To bring you to the Seating Room alone. Immediately."

"Did he also tell you to leave a scratch on his son?" I asked, my voice devoid of any accent. I'd slipped into the affect of the rich, spoiled, powerful Heir to the Arkasva and Imperator.

Baynan flinched. He realized the line he'd crossed, though this line had been blurring since I'd become a soturion. He'd seen my father strike me, bind me, humiliate me. They all had. And as my father's punishments became more severe, as I'd become a target in the Katurium at his behest, his soturi had taken it as an allowance to be rougher with me, as if my father's mistreatment gave them permission to hurt me, too.

But it hadn't. My father didn't like his things to be touched. Not if he wasn't present to order the harm or do the harming himself. He always seemed torn between wanting to hurt me, and wanting me to be respected by others—it just depended on the current mood he was in, and which outcome better suited his ego.

"You'll be lashed if I find a single mark on His Grace," Bowen threatened. "We yield to the Imperator's command. You've made your summons. So, take your Godsdamned hand off him and let him step outside."

The soturi released me at once, but they each took a step closer, ensuring I didn't escape, at least, not in the traditional way.

I sucked in my breath, biting the inner corner of my cheek. I had to stay calm. To remain in control. To remain *here*.

Inhale. Exhale.

My father didn't know about the gryphon. He couldn't. The soturi would have grabbed Artem by now as well, and they hadn't. But I was sure I'd been caught anyway on another charge, on a far greater crime. He knew I'd used my vorakh. He knew I'd disobeyed him, let my emotions take over. And now I was going to pay.

THE EMPIRE OF LUMERIA

There are twelve countries united under the Lumerian Empire. The 12 Ruling Kavim of Lumeria Nutavia. Each country is ruled by an Arkasva, the High Lord or Lady of the ruling Ka.

All twelve countries submit to the rule and law of the Emperor. Each Arkasva also answers to an Imperator, one Arkasva with jurisdiction over each country in either the Northern or Southern hemispheres of the Empire.

In addition to the Emperor's rule, twelve senators, one from each country (may not be a member of the ruling Ka) fill the twelve seats of the Senate. The roles of Imperator and Emperor are lifelong appointments. They may not be passed onto family members. Imperators and Emperors must be elected by the ruling Kavim. Kavim may not submit a candidate for either role if the previous Imperator or Emperor belonged to their Ka.

Imperators may keep their ties to their Ka and rule in their country. An Emperor will lose their Ka upon anointing and must be like a father or mother to all Lumerians.

EMPIRIC CHAIN OF COMMAND
EMPEROR THEOTIS, HIGH LORD OF LUMERIA NUTAVIA

The Emperor rules over the entire Empire, from its capitol, Numeria. The Emperor oversees the running of the Senate, and the twelve countries united under the Empire.

Devon Hart, Imperator to the North
The Imperator of the North is an Arkasva who rules not only their country, but oversees rule of the remaining five countries belonging to the North. His rule includes the following countries currently by the following Kavim:

Glemaria, Ka Hart
Payunmar, Ka Valyan
Hartavia, Ka Taria
Ereztia, Ka Sephiron
Aravia, Ka Lumerin
Sindhuvine, Ka Kether

Avery Kormac, Imperator to the South
The Imperator of the South is an Arkasva who rules not only their country, but oversees rule of the remaining five countries belonging to the North. The sitting Imperator is also nephew to

the Emperor. His rule includes the following countries currently being ruled by the following Kavim:

Bamaria, Ka Batavia

Korteria, Ka Kormac

Elyria, Ka Elys (previously Ka Azria)

Damara, Ka Daquataine

Lethea, Ka Maras

Cretanya, Ka Zarine

The Immortal Afeyan Courts*

The Sun Court: El Zandria, ruled by King RaKanam

The Moon Court: Khemet, ruled by Queen Ma'Nia

The Star Court: Night Lands, ruled by Queen Ishtara

Afeyan Courts are not considered part of the Lumerian Empire, nor do they submit to the Emperor, however, history, prior treaties, and trade agreements have kept the courts at peace, and working together. They are the only two groups to have shared life on the continent of Lumeria Matavia.

THE BAMARIAN COUNCIL

Each of the twelve countries in the Lumerian Empire includes a 12-member council comprised of members of the nobility to assist the Arkasva in ruling and decision-making.

The Bamarian Council includes the following:

Role, Name

Arkasva, Harren Batavia

Master of the Horse, Eathan Ezara

Arkturion, Aemon Melvik

Turion, Dairen Melvik

Arkmage, Kolaya Scholar

Master of Education, Arianna Batavia

Master of Spies, Sila Shavo

Master of Finance, Romula Grey

Master of Law, Kiera Ezara

Naturion, Dagana Scholar

Senator, Janvi Elys

Master of Peace, Brenna Corra

TITLES AND FORMS OF ADDRESS

Arkasva (Ark-kas-va): Ruler of the country, literally translates as the "will of the highest soul."

Arkasvim (Ark-kas-veem): Plural of Arkasva

Arkturion (Ark-tor-ree-an): Warlord for the country, general of their soturi/army.

Imperator: A miniature Emperor. The Empire always has two Imperators, one for the Northern Hemisphere, one for the South. The Imperator will also be the arkasva of their country, they have jurisdiction over their hemisphere but also act as a voice and direct messenger between each Arkasva and the Emperor.

Emperor: Ruler of all twelve countries in the Lumerian Empire. The Emperor is elected by the ruling arkasvim. They are appointed for life. Once an Emperor or Empress dies, the Kavim must elect a new ruler. The Emperor must renounce their Ka when anointed, but no Ka may produce an Emperor/Empress twice in a row.

Heir Apparent: Title given to the eldest child or heir of the Arkasva. The next in line to the Seat of Power or First from the Seat.

Soturion: Soldier, magically enhanced warrior. A Lumerian who can transmute magic through their body. May be used as a form of address for a non-noble.

Turion: Commander, may lead legions of soturi, must answer to their Arkturion.

Mage: A Lumerian who transmutes magic through spells. A stave is used to focus their magic. The more focus one has, the less a stave is needed, but the more magic one can use, the larger the stave may need to be. Arkmages (the high mages) tend to have staves as tall as them.

Novice: The term used to describe a soturion or mage who is in the beginning of their learning to become an anointed mage or soturion.

Apprentice: The term used to describe a soturion or mage who has passed their first three years of training. As an apprentice their time is divided between their own studies and teaching the novice they are bound to. This is done to strengthen the power of Kashonim, and because of the Bamarian philosophy that teaching a subject is the best way to learn and master a subject.

Lady: Formal address for a female, or female-identifying member of the nobility.

Lord: Formal address for a male, or male-identifying member of the nobility.

Your Grace: Formal address for any member of the ruling Ka. Anyone who is in line to the Seat of Power must be addressed so, including the Arkasva. A noble may only be addressed as "your grace" if they are in line to the Seat.

Your Highness: Reserved as formal address only for the member of Lumerian nobility serving as imperator. The term of address has also been adopted by the Afeyan Star Court.

Your Majesty: Used only for the Emperor or Empress. Previously used for the kings and queens of Lumeria Matavia.

This can also be applied to the King and Queen of the Afeyan Sun and Moon Courts.

GLOSSARY

Names:

Lyriana Batavia (Leer-ree-ana Ba-tah-via): Third in line to the Seat of Power in Bamaria

Morgana Batavia (Mor-ga-na Ba-tah-via): Second in line to the Seat of Power in Bamaria

Meera Batavia (Mee-ra Ba-tah-via): First in line to the Seat of Power in Bamaria (Heir Apparent)

Naria Batavia (Nar-ria Ba-tah-via): Niece to the Arkasva, not in line to the Seat

Arianna Batavia (Ar-ree-ana Ba-tah-via): Sister-in-law to the Arkasva, previously third in line to Seat, Master of Education on the Council of Bamaria

Aemon Melvik (Ae-mon Mel-vik): Warlord of Bamaria, Arkturion on the Council of Bamaria

Rhyan Hart (Ry-an Hart): Forsworn and exiled from Glemaria. Previously was in first in line to the Seat of Power (Heir Apparent)

Haleika Grey (Hal-eye-ka Gray): Tristan's cousin, and one of the few friends and allies Lyr has in the Soturion Academy

Auriel (Or-ree-el): Original Guardian of the Valalumir in

Heaven, stole the light to bring to Earth where it turned into a crystal before shattering at the time of the Drowning

Asherah (A-sher-ah): Original Guardian of the Valalumir in Heaven. She was banished to Earth as a mortal after her affair with Auriel was discovered.

Mercurial (Mer-cure-ree-el): An immortal Afeya, First Messenger of her Highness Queen Ishtara, High Lady of the Night Lands

Moriel (Mor-ree-el): Original Guardian of the Valalumir in Heaven. He reported Auriel and Asherah's affair to the Council of 44 leading to Asherah's banishment, Auriel's theft of the light, and its subsequent destruction. He was banished to Earth where he allied with the akadim in the war that led to the Drowning.

Theotis (Thee-otis): Current Emperor of Lumeria Nutavia. Theotis was previously from Korteria, and a noble of Ka Kormac. His nephew, Avery Kormac, is the current Imperator to the Southern hemisphere of the Empire, and Arkasva to Korteria.

Avery Kormac (Ae-very Core-mac): Nephew to the Emperor, as Imperator, he rules over the six southern countries of the Empire, as well as ruling Korteria as the Arkasva.

Afeya (Ah-fay-ah): Immortal Lumerians who survived the Drowning. Prior to, Afeya were non-distinguishable from other Lumerians in Lumeria Matavia. They were descended from the Gods and Goddesses, trapped in the mortal coil. But they refused the request to join the war efforts. Some sources believe they allied with Moriel's forces and the akadim. When the Valalumir shattered, they were cursed to live forever, unable to return to their home, be relieved of life, or touch or perform magic—unless asked to by another.

Places:

Lumeria (Lu-mair-ria): The name of continent where Gods and Goddesses first incarnated until it sank into the Lumerian Ocean in the Drowning.

Matavia (Ma-tah-via): Motherland. When used with Lumeria, it refers to the continent that sank.

Nutavia (New-tah-via): New land. When used with Lumeria, it refers to the Empire forged after the Drowning by those who survived and made it to Bamaria—previously Dobra.

Bamaria (Ba-mar-ria): Southernmost country of the Lumerian Empire, home of the South's most prestigious University and the Great Library. Ruled by Ka Batavia.

Korteria (Kor-ter-ria): Westernmost country in the Empire. Magic is least effective in their mountains, but Korteria does have access to Starfire for Lumerian weapons. Ruled by Ka Kormac.

Elyria (El-leer-ria): Historically ruled by Ka Azria, rulership has now passed to Ka Elys, originally nobility from Bamaria.

Lethea (Lee-thee-a): The only part of the Empire located in the Lumerian Ocean. Ruled by Ka Maras, this is the country where criminals stripped of powers, or accused of vorakh are sent for imprisonment. The expression "Farther than Lethea" comes from the fact that there is nothing but ocean beyond the island. Due to the Drowning, the idea of going past the island is akin to losing one's mind.

Damara (Da-mar-ra): A Southern country known for strong warriors, ruled by Ka Daquataine.

Glemaria (Gleh-mar-ria): Northernmost country of the Empire, ruled by Ka Hart. Imperator Devon Hart is the Arkasva and Imperator to the North. Rhyan Hart was previously first in line to the Seat.

Prominent Creatures of the Old World Known to Have Survived the Drowning:

Seraphim (Ser-a-feem): Birds with wings of gold, they resemble a cross between an eagle and a dove. Seraphim are peaceful creatures, sacred in Bamaria, and most often used for transport across the Lumerian Empire. Though delicate in appearance, they are extremely strong and can carry loads of up ten people over short distances. Seraphim all prefer warmer climates and are rarely found in the northernmost part of the Empire.

Ashvan: Flying horses. These are the only sky creatures that do not possess wings. Their flight comes from magic contained in their hooves. Once an ashvan picks up speed, their magic will create small temporary pathways to run upon. Technically, ashvan cannot fly, but are running on magic pathways that appear and vanish once stepped upon. Residue of the magic is left behind, creating streaks behind them, but these fade within seconds.

Nahashim: Snakes with the ability to grow and shrink at will, able to fit into any size space for the purposes of seeking. Anything lost or desired can almost always be found by a nahashim. Their scales remain almost burning hot and they prefer to live near the water. Most nahashim are bred on Lethea, the country furthest out into the ocean, closest to the original location of Lumeria Matavia.

Gryphon (Grif-in): Sky creatures that are half eagle, half lion. Extremely large, these animals can be taken into battle, preferring mountains and colder climates. They replace seraphim and ashvan in the northernmost parts of the Lumerian Empire. They may carry far heavier loads than seraphim.

Akadim (A-ka-deem): The most feared of all creatures, literally bodies without souls. Akadim kill by eating the soul of their victims. The demonic creatures were previously Lumerians transformed. Akadim grow to be twice the size of a Lumerian and gain five times the strength of a soturion. Immortal as long as they continue to feed on souls, these creatures are impervious to Lumerian magic. Akadim are weakened by the sun and tend to live in the Northern Hemisphere.

Water Dragon: Dragons with blue scales that live deep in the Lumerian Ocean. Previously spending their time equally between land and water, all water dragons have taken to the Lumerian Ocean and are usually spotted closer to Lethea.

Agnavim (Ahg-naw-veem): Rarely sighted in Lumerian lands. These red birds with wings made of pure flame favor the lands occupied by the Afeyan Star Court. Lumerians have been unable to tame them since the Drowning.

Terms/Items:

Birth Bind/Binding: Unlike a traditional bind which includes a spell that ties a rope around a Lumerian to keep them from touching their power, or restricting their physical ability to move a Birth Bind leaves no mark. A Binding is temporary, and can have more or less strength and heat depending on the mage casting the spell. A Birth Bind is given to all Lumerians in their first year of life, a spell that will keep them from accessing their magic power whenever it develops. All Lumerians develop their magic along with puberty. The Birth Bind may only be removed after the Lumerian has turned nineteen, the age of adulthood.

Dagger: Ceremonial weapon given to soturi. The dagger has no special power on its own as the magic of a soturion is transmuted through their body.

Ka (Kah): Soul. A Ka is a soul tribe or family.

Kashonim (Ka-show-neem): Ancestral lineage and link of power. Calling on Kashonim allows you to absorb the power of your lineage, but depending on the situation, usage can be dangerous. For one, it can be an overwhelming amount of power that leaves you unconscious if you come from a long lineage, or a particularly powerful one. Two, it has the potential to weaken the mages or soturi the caller is drawing from. It is also illegal to use against fellow students.

Kavim (Ka-veem): Plural of Ka. A Ka can be likened to a soul tribe or family. When marriages occur, either member of the union may take on the name of their significant other's Ka. Typically, the Ka with more prestige or nobility will be used thus ensuring the most powerful Kavim continue to grow.

Laurel of the Arkasva (Lor-el of the Ar-kas-va): A golden circlet like a crown worn by the Arkasva. The Arkasva replaced the title of King and Queen in Lumeria Matavia, and the Laurel replaced the crown though they are held in the same high esteem.

Seat of Power: Akin to a throne. Thrones were replaced by Seats in Lumeria Nutavia, as many members of royalty were blamed by the citizens of Lumeria for the Drowning. Much as a monarch may have a throne room, the Arkasvim have a Seating Room. The Arkasva typically has a Seat of Power in their Seating Room in their Ka's fortress, and another in their temple.

Stave: Made of twisted moon and sun wood, the stave transmutes magic created by mages. A stave is not needed to perform magic, but greatly focuses and strengthens it. More magic being transmuted may require a larger stave.

Vadati (Va-dah-tee): Stones that allow Lumerians to hear and speak to each other over vast distances. Most of these stones were lost in the Drowning. The Empire now keeps a strict registry of each known stone.

Valalumir (Val-la-loo-meer): The sacred light of Heaven that began the Celestial War which began in Heaven and ended with the Drowning. The light was guarded by seven Gods and Goddesses until Asherah and Auriel's affair. Asherah was banished to become mortal, and Auriel fell to bring her the light. Part of the light went into Asherah before it crystalized. When the war ended, the Valalumir shattered in seven pieces—all lost in the Drowning.

Valya (Val-yah): The sacred text of recounting the history of the Lumerian people up until the Drowning. There are multiple valyas recorded, each with slight variations, but the Mar Valya is the standard. Another popular translation is the Tavia Valya which is believed to have been better preserved than the Mar Valya after the Drowning, but was never made into the standard for copying. Slight changes or possible effects of water damage offer different insights into Auriel's initial meeting with Asherah.

Vorakh (Vor-rock): Taboo, forbidden powers. Three magical abilities that faded after the Drowning are considered illegal: visions, mind-reading, and traveling by mind. Vorakh can be translated as "gift from the Gods" in High Lumerian, but is now translated as "curse from the Gods."

LUMERIAN RIGHTS OF PASSAGE

Revelation Ceremony: All Lumerians are given a Birth Bind in their first year of life, a spell that will keep them from accessing their magic power whenever it develops. All Lumerians develop their magic along with puberty. **The Birth Bind** may only be removed after the Lumerian has turned nineteen, the age of adulthood. Any Lumerian who is nineteen may participate in the Revelation Ceremony that year, celebrated on Auriel's Feast Day. At this time, their binding is removed by an Arkmage, and they may choose whether they will become a mage and be offered a stave, or a soturion and receive a dagger. The Arkmage will cut each participant to begin an oath that completes itself in the Oath Ceremony. Participants traditionally wear white robes which are discarded after their choice is made. A cut is made to the left wrist for a soturion, and their oath is made by dripping their blood into fire. A cut is made to the right wrist for a mage, and their oath is made by dripping their blood into water.

Oath Ceremony: Following the decision to become a mage or soturion, every Lumerian will become part of a Kashonim, or lineage. This allows them greater access to power in times of need, as well as continues to establish bonds across the Kavim and keep the Empire united. During the Oath Ceremony, every mage and soturion becomes a novice, and is bound to an apprentice. Once the oath is sworn, the novice has access to the powers of the apprentice's entire living lineage. The apprentice is also duty-bound to teach the novice all they know. Romantic relationships are strongly discouraged between mage apprentice and novices.

Romantic relationships are strictly forbidden between apprentice and novice soturi as this can cause interruptions to their duties to fight and protect. Participants traditionally wear black robes which are burned before their apprentice dresses them in their new attire.

Anointing: After an apprentice completes their training, they will be anointed, and become a full-fledged member of Lumerian society. An anointed mage or soturion is one who has completed their training. Anointing ceremonies will also be performed anytime a Lumerian rises in rank, for example an Heir becoming Arkasva, or an Arkasva becoming Imperator or Emperor. Anointings signify a life-long role.

Acknowledgments

I have to tell you that writing a novella wasn't on my 2022 bingo card. Or my life bingo card. Yet here I am. I am not someone who thinks in terms of short. When I think of story, I think of all the parts, how epic it can be and how many books it will take to write. So I felt pretty confident in the fact that I would never ever write a novella. But if you take that personality trait and go back to the origin of Solstice, which was just a scene, I suppose this all makes sense (and actually, I was right in the end...I didn't write a *novella*).

Solstice's creation all began when you, dear readers, started requesting not just the full scene of Rhyan and Lyr's first kiss, but to see it in his POV. And I said yes. But Rhyan was so moody that summer, and had so many reasons for ignoring Lyr before that night that I realized pretty quickly, this wasn't just a scene, but a story. One I guess Rhyan really wanted me to tell, because he kept telling me things that were not about that night. Before I knew it, I was handing over the first two chapters of my "short story" to Marcella who was still recovering from hosting the launch of Guardian of the Drowned Empire with me. When I asked her if she'd read them for feedback, her response was, "Frankie, you know short stories don't have chapters." To which I replied, "So?" And she agreed to look at the chapters if I would stop living in denial and admit I was actually writing a novella.

So I did. And here we are. Except, as you now know, I wrote a novel. But whatever.

This one was scary to share as it was so different from

Daughter and Guardian. New narrator, new time period, and we got to spend time in some company that we don't usually get too close to (who maybe aren't the most pleasant people to be around), as well as a cast of new characters, and a lot less Lyr. But I'm really glad I spent some time here, deepening even my own understanding of Rhyan before I dive deeper into the main series. And this one became a lot more personal than even I was expecting. So thank you for being on this little detour in the journey with me.

As always, I couldn't get through a book without the price-less feedback of Donna Kuzma, and your impeccable and brutal critiques.

Asha Venkataraman, I am forever grateful for your beta reading and enthusiasm, and years of friendship.

Marcella Haddad for helping me capture Rhyan's distinctive voice from the start, and believing I could do this.

Danielle Dyal, for once again some quick, and kick-butt copy-editing.

Stefanie Saw, for the amazing cover design! After some back and forth on the concept you nailed it and I literally gasped when I saw the tree.

Steve Kuzma, thank you for allowing me to not have to worry about the website like ever. Because I never want to do that.

Mom, for always supporting my writing.

Julie for all of your support, and technical uploading assistance—I would be lost without you.

Elissa, for staying on top of all the data analysis and being as excited as I am.

Eva, for reading and supporting.

Michael, for always supporting.

Miguel, for always checking in.

Dylan, Blake, Hannah, and Dani, because I will always thank you no matter what.

For the ARC Team for being willing to try something a little outside of the box that wasn't actually the next book in the story (which I know you all want). Thank you, thank you, thank you!

And of course for Forsworn Mayhem, the Street Team for being so enthusiastic and supportive and really taking a load off my shoulders as I headed into launch mode (I can't thank you all enough for everything you're doing and for really just existing). Huge thanks to: Christine Stewart, Emma Reece, Heather Aspero, Marisa Schindler, Sandra Jean Glazebrook, Kyla Clarkston, Emma Russell, Victoria Marie Webb, Kristianna Weppler, Mercurial's Queen, Brianne Glickman, Emily Carlisle, Jade Lawson, Courtney Washburn, Tasha Jenkins, Heather Corrales, Justine Caylor, Yaneth Aguirre, Audra Jones, Alisa Huntington, Megan Cristofaro, Zoë J. OsikCéline Yzewyn, Katie Hunsberger, Mandy Carleton, Kayleigh Foland, Katie Mazza, Lauren Richards, Lara Kine, Marisa Sevenski, Sarah Heifetz, Courtney Stosser, Emily Kordys, Raqui Cobo-Flores, Kayla Hjelmstad, Cynthia Williams, Bekah Abraham, Iliana Katana, Priscilla Osorno, Brynly Kapelanski, Meghan Hughes, Nadia Larumbe, Madi Healey, Alina Heras, Erin Smith, Brittany Crain, Tifany Ness, Takecia Bright, Olivia Baumgartner, Maria Schmelz, Alexandra Marshall, Shana Heinrich, Maggie Siciliano, Emily Blakeslee, Joyce Fernandez, Sam Love, Kelsey Rhodes.

All right, here we go. See you all after Lady of the Drowned Empire!

Love,

Frankie

ALSO BY FRANKIE DIANE MALLIS

ABOUT THE AUTHOR

Frankie Diane Mallis lives outside of Philadelphia where she is an award-winning university professor. When not writing or teaching, she practices yoga and belly dance and can usually be found baking gluten free desserts. The Drowned Empire Series is her debut fantasy romance series. Visit www.frankiediane-mallis.com to learn more, and join the newsletter. Follow Frankie on Instagram @frankiediane, and on TikTok @frankiedi-anebooks.